FALLING FOR THE BILLIONAIRE DOC

—

AMY RUTTAN

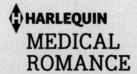

MEDICAL ROMANCE

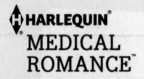

HARLEQUIN®
MEDICAL ROMANCE™

Recycling programs for this product may not exist in your area.

ISBN-13: 978-1-335-40874-7

Falling for the Billionaire Doc

Copyright © 2021 by Amy Ruttan

Harlequin Enterprises ULC
22 Adelaide St. West, 40th Floor
Toronto, Ontario M5H 4E3, Canada
www.Harlequin.com

Printed in U.S.A.

Henry glanced at her and her heart skipped a beat. "You did look really pretty tonight."

"Thank you." Heat flooded her cheeks.

Kiera's pulse was thundering in her ears as they sat there next to each other in the car. She shivered.

"Here." His arm slipped around her, pulling her close. She knew she should push him away, but his arm felt nice and she stopped shivering.

And she couldn't remember the last time she'd felt something like this.

It felt good.

What was she doing?

She looked over at him. Her body was humming with anticipation. Her mouth was dry, and her breathing was fast as their gazes locked.

And before she could stop herself, she became swept up in something.

Something she didn't quite know how to control and something that she couldn't stop. And she wasn't completely sure that she wanted to stop it.

Dear Reader,

Thank you for picking up a copy of Kiera and Henry's story, *Falling for the Billionaire Doc*.

This book came about because I wanted to virtually travel somewhere and Colorado was on my bucket list.

Kiera is trying desperately to save the hospital she works at. She's tired of the rich getting richer and the poor struggling, and she knows about struggling. The only thing standing in her way is a governor, but instead of the governor coming to talk to her, he sends his son.

Henry is tired of his father's politics, but his father helped him out and Henry owes him. He will put an end to the protests during his father's election year and be released from the debt he owes.

As soon as Kiera and Henry meet, sparks fly... and there's no stopping love once it decides to hit, even if both parties are unwilling to open their hearts again.

I hope you enjoy Kiera and Henry's story.

I love hearing from readers, so please drop by my website, www.amyruttan.com, or give me a shout on Twitter, @ruttanamy.

With warmest wishes,

Amy Ruttan

Born and raised just outside Toronto, Ontario, **Amy Ruttan** fled the big city to settle down with the country boy of her dreams. After the birth of her second child, Amy was lucky enough to realize her lifelong dream of becoming a romance author. When she's not furiously typing away at her computer, she's mom to three wonderful children, who use her as a personal taxi and chef.

Books by Amy Ruttan

Harlequin Medical Romance

First Response
Pregnant with the Paramedic's Baby

Cinderellas to Royal Brides
Royal Doc's Secret Heir

NY Doc Under the Northern Lights
Carrying the Surgeon's Baby
The Surgeon's Convenient Husband
Baby Bombshell for the Doctor Prince
Reunited with Her Hot-Shot Surgeon
A Reunion, a Wedding, a Family
Twin Surprise for the Baby Doctor

Visit the Author Profile page
at Harlequin.com for more titles.

For Christine and Sif,
for the inspiration and the name!

CHAPTER ONE

FREAKING COLD.

Dr. Henry Blake scowled up at the first few flakes of snow swirling around in the air. He hated the cold. He hated the fresh air, the woods and the windchill, and he scowled up at the cloud-covered sky, hoping he could melt every single last stupid snowflake that was falling down.

Why am I here again?

And then he distinctly remembered why he was back in Colorado in the bitter cold of February. He remembered why he had been dragged away from his warm, beautiful beachfront home in Los Angeles—to deal with a problem at his father's request.

He had been born in Aspen, Colorado. It was where his father was the governor and sat on the boards of many hospitals in the state. Even though it was Henry's birthplace, his family didn't spend much time here. His parents were elite and wealthy, and only came to Aspen when the powder was fresh so they could rub elbows with the rich and famous.

His parents preferred Denver, DC or New York City. Basically, wherever their powerful friends were, his parents weren't far behind.

Whereas he had always been left alone.

Alone in a large house in Denver.

Alone at boarding school for the holidays.

Alone and scared.

Henry didn't have many fond memories of Colorado.

Or the winter. He hated how coming back unpacked feelings he kept carefully locked away.

He had returned only because he sat on the board of Aspen Grace Memorial Hospital, one of the hospitals his father had invested a lot of money in.

And then there was the debt Henry owed to his father. One he was sure he could never really repay. One that left him beholden to the man who was biologically his father, but emotionally meant nothing to him.

Henry hated owing anyone anything, and he did care about the hospitals he was involved in.

Even if it necessitated being in Colorado and subjected to the winter he loathed so much.

His father had big plans for the future of Aspen Grace Memorial. But, apparently, there was a problem in going forward with tearing down the old and building the new.

And that problem was one Dr. Brown. Henry knew nothing about her although he had read a couple of articles she'd written in medical journals.

She was smart, a good surgeon, but very, very vocal about her displeasure with his father and the board of directors.

She was the reason he was back in Colorado. She'd been ignoring his calls and emails. Now he had to come and meet her face-to-face. Which annoyed him all the more.

More than the cold weather.

Henry jammed his hands into the pockets of his coat, trying to hunker down under his scarf as the wind shifted and blew a blast of snow straight into his face.

"You know, you should've dressed a bit better, Dr. Baker. This isn't LA."

Henry glared at his father's driver, who had pulled up to meet him at his parents' private hangar. While he was glad of the private plane and the ride, he couldn't help but be irritated by the reason for it.

You owe me, his father had snarled.

I owe you nothing, Henry had said. *Send someone else to deal with Dr. Brown.*

His father had glared at him. *Remember all*

those gambling debts? Remember how you walked away from medicine and almost ruined your career in Los Angeles, how we supported you after Michelle died and how we covered up all your indiscretions.

A chill had run down his spine. *Yes.*

You owe me this. I saved your career. Sent you to the finest schools. You can deal with this problem. I can't do this with the election coming up.

Fine, but after I do this we're done. No more holding anything over my head.

Very well.

What would you have me do?

His father had shrugged. *Seduce her for all I care. Just shut it down.*

Henry had no plans to seduce Dr. Brown. Woo her maybe, charm her, but that was it.

And he hoped this one last favor would put an ending to owing his father.

To have it brought up every time he saw him.

Then Henry could be free.

Can you ever really be free?

"I won't be in the area long, and I have no plans for frolicking outside," Henry grumbled. "I have work waiting for me in Los Angeles. I only came to deal with Dr. Brown and get the demolition back on schedule."

His father's driver, Mike, laughed, and Henry

had a sinking feeling in the pit of his stomach, which he ignored as he climbed into the back of his parents' luxury sedan, thankful for the heated seats.

Henry wasn't going to stay long. A week tops.

All he had to do was deal with Dr. Brown, listen to her issues and get everything back on track to build Aspen Grace Memorial into a cutting edge private medical facility. Then he could return to his beach house.

What's waiting for you there?

He shook the thought away. He needed to focus on the task at hand.

AGMH was run-down.

It was overcrowded and didn't serve the community. Tourists didn't feel safe using the hospital. They didn't like it.

The hospital board wasn't planning on doing away with the hospital completely. The board was going to build something better in its place.

Something that would bring in lots of money.

Only Dr. Brown didn't see it that way and she was protesting. Handing out flyers, stopping construction. Attending meetings at city hall to try to put a stop to it. It was slowing down the progress.

Henry really didn't care one way or another.

His father did, though.

So that's why he was here.

He owed his parents this. They had saved his life and reputation after Michelle died; however, after Henry dealt with this, he was done.

He'd sell his shares in the hospitals and cut ties with his parents.

He had spent far too many years trying to please them, hoping they'd love him, when it was clear they never would.

The only person who had ever loved him was Michelle and she was gone.

Henry sighed.

It was inevitable that his mother would soon come to see him, and no doubt she'd start harassing him about settling down and the family image. His parents hated his lifestyle of dating women in Los Angeles for short stints. It looked bad for their good family name.

The wholesome image his father promoted didn't seem exactly truthful when there was an unsettled son dating all the wrong kind of women.

If only the general public knew his real father.

His father was not a good family man.

His father was a charlatan.

Of course, the one time he had been serious with someone she hadn't come from the right family. She hadn't been good enough.

She'd been good enough for him, though, and he smiled as he thought about her.

She'd been gone for eight years, but the hole in his heart remained.

Michelle had been the first person to get through the walls he'd built as a child to protect his heart. The first person to truly love him, and he had adored her.

He had imagined a life, marriage, children with her, and in one tragic instance it had all been snatched away. He would never go through that pain again.

And he was tired of his parents throwing what they thought of as respectable women at him. All he wanted was to be left alone.

Was that too much to ask?

So now he was in Aspen to deal with Dr. Kiera Brown so that his father didn't have to, and with any luck this would be the end of it. The end of his father holding his indiscretions over his head.

Constantly reminding him how much he owed him.

How Henry wasn't good enough.

This was the last thing he would do for his father.

Henry knew, in his father's eyes, he'd never be that perfect son.

The one time he had come close to being that was Michelle. Only Michelle had thought he was worthy of love. Even that had gone spectacularly wrong when she had died following an accident. The only good thing in his life had been taken away eight years ago.

It still stung.

It still hurt after all this time.

Michelle had been his world. The only woman he had ever trusted. The only woman who hadn't wanted anything from him in return for his love.

She had loved Henry for himself. When Henry had been with her, he had forgotten all those sad, lonely years as a child.

She had given him hope.

Michelle had been his everything. Michelle and medicine. They had never failed him.

Medicine had made him happy at one time. Just like it had made Michelle happy, too, but in a way, in the end, medicine had failed Michelle.

And now Henry was jaded with life, with work.

He'd lost passion for everything.

He just wanted to be back in California and be left alone.

That's all he wanted.

He scowled the closer they got to town. The traffic was backed up and the mountains surrounding the town were covered with skiers.

It was the height of the tourist season.

This wasn't the time of year he liked being

in Aspen. He had a condo here he rarely visited. He'd come back maybe three times since he bought it, and that was in the summer. He often thought he should sell it, but he was glad he had it now. Hotels would be booked solid, they would be crowded and noisy, and there was no way he was staying at his parents' place.

He had enough bad memories of that house.

Is there any time of year you like to be in Colorado?

Michelle had loved Colorado. Though he hadn't understood why, if it had made her happy he would have stayed.

He'd met Michelle in Denver.

Why do you want to settle down in Colorado? he'd asked her. *Los Angeles is more exciting!*

You're from Colorado, she'd teased.

Exactly. He had smiled and kissed her. *Take it from me. There's nothing great about living in the mountains.*

I love the mountains. I grew up in Salt Lake City, Utah. I'm used to life elevated. Her blue eyes had sparkled. *Don't you think this would be a great place to raise a family?*

One day, he'd grumbled.

Exactly. She had wrapped her arms around him. *We'll both have thriving practices. We could stay here. I know you hate living in the shadow of your parents, but I love Colorado.*

We can live in Denver and take our kids skiing in Aspen, we'll stay at your parents' ski lodge and in the summer we can go back to Salt Lake City to see my family or even drive up to Yellowstone.

He'd groaned. *I forgot you're an outdoorsy person.*

And you love me for it.

Michelle had been right. He *had* loved her for it. And it hurt his heart, even eight years later, when he thought of her. When he let those thoughts creep through into his mind. Of the life they could've had together. Maybe he would've liked Colorado more, Aspen more, if he had been with her.

If they'd had the family they planned on.

That had all been taken away from him.

Snatched cruelly.

He'd been back, but rarely.

And it was because he had let those thoughts creep into his head that he was so angry that he had been forced to come here and deal with this. At least he was almost free of his parents.

Mike turned down a street.

"Where are we going?" Henry asked.

"To the construction site," Mike responded.

"I was supposed to head to the hospital. That's where I was going to have my meeting with the heads of the departments and Dr. Brown."

"Dr. Brown is not at the hospital. I called ahead, Dr. Baker. She's at the construction site and she's protesting."

"She's protesting?"

Mike nodded. "I figured you wanted to speak with her first. In fact, I have instructions from your father to put an end to any kind of demonstration at the construction site. He doesn't want the police involved."

"Of course not," Henry grumbled to himself under his breath.

His father wouldn't want there to be a scene. His father abhorred the press unless it was good publicity.

A doctor campaigning at a new hospital site was not good publicity.

Of course, neither were his countless dates with Los Angeles glitterati. Even though none of those dates were ever serious. The women wanted something from him and he from them. His father hated the tabloid shots of Henry. And just thinking of that, he smiled briefly to himself.

Mike pulled in close to the work site, boarded up for the winter but ready for construction in the spring. Henry was expecting to see more people with Dr. Brown because he knew there were others who didn't want AGMH to shut down. He was bracing himself for the worst and was taken aback when he didn't see a horde of protestors.

It was just one lone woman, bundled up against the cold, holding a sign that had a picture of his father's face with devil horns and dollar signs painted on it.

In glitter.

Portraying his father's greed.

She wasn't wrong. His father didn't value much; nor did his mother, which was something he had learned as a child being raised by servants and sent away to boarding school.

Henry tried to wipe the smile off his face, but it was hard not to laugh. It was kind of absurd—and admirable. He looked up and saw in the rearview mirror that Mike's eyes were twinkling with mirth, too.

"So this is Dr. Brown?" Henry asked.

"Yep." Mike nodded.

"I won't be long." Henry opened the door and pulled his coat tight as a blast of cold wind blew down from the mountain against him.

He slammed the door and Dr. Brown paused, but didn't drop her hold on the sign. The biting wind helped him to keep a straight face. So that was something.

"Dr. Brown?" he asked, stepping closer.

All he could see were two brilliant green eyes, staring back at him over a thick scarf that was wound around her face and under a knit beanie that was jammed on the top of her head.

"Yes?"

"I'm Dr. Baker. We were supposed to have a meeting at AGMH."

She rolled her eyes. "I don't need a meeting with the governor's son on my day off. I have more important things to do."

"What? Being the only one marching in the middle of a snowstorm campaigning against a new hospital?"

Those green eyes narrowed. "Exactly. Although, this is hardly a snowstorm."

"You do know that I sit on the board of directors for AGMH. I am technically your boss." He shivered against another blast of bitterly cold wind.

"Yes, but I'm not on call. I'm not on duty today, and the last time I checked it was my right to demonstrate wherever I want. So if you'll excuse me…" She hoisted the sign up further and continued her march.

She wasn't wrong, but he was annoyed just the same. This was not going to be easy.

"What're you hoping to accomplish?" he shouted over the wind.

She turned and looked back at him. "Are you willing to discuss terms?"

No.

That wasn't his position, but right now he wanted to get out of the cold and have a rational meeting. His father had made it clear he didn't want attention drawn to this situation. That's all he had to do. Get her to stop this, and he could go back to his life in Los Angeles.

What life?

"Sure," Henry agreed, lying through his teeth.

There was nothing really to discuss. He was going to tell her to end her foolish protest or find somewhere else to work. It was as simple as that.

Dr. Brown lowered her sign. "Fine. I'll go with you, and we can talk about this and see if we can come to some kind of resolution."

"I'm giving you a drive?" he questioned as she marched past him toward the car.

"I walked here. My house isn't far. We can go there if you'd like, but I figured you'd want to discuss things in the boardroom in the hospital. You know, exert power over your lackeys."

What was her problem?

And now he understood why Mike was laughing and why his father was in such a tizzy and hadn't wanted to deal with Dr. Brown himself.

Rock. Meet hard place.

"Fine," he said through gritted teeth. "We'll go to the hospital."

She nodded. "You know, you really should be wearing a thicker coat. This is winter, after all."

Henry clenched his fists.

Maybe this wasn't going to be easy at all. He climbed into the back of the car while Mike helped Dr. Brown wrestle her sign into the trunk and then held the door open for her as she slid in.

She was still wearing her hat and scarf.

"You have the heat cranked in here," she remarked.

"As you said. It's winter."

Dr. Brown pulled off her hat and a cascade of red hair tumbled out. He could hear the electric shock of static electricity, and some of her hair stood on end.

Then she unwound the scarf from around her face, and he was in absolute awe when he laid eyes on her.

Henry didn't know quite what he'd been expecting, but he knew it hadn't been someone so young. The Dr. Kiera Brown he'd been briefed on was not the person he thought she'd be.

He had expected a surgeon more around his father's age, given her lists of accomplishments. Not this gorgeous, vibrant woman sitting in front of him.

Not someone so beautiful.

There was a zing of something, a spark that

warmed his blood, even in the bitter cold. Something he hadn't felt in a long time.

He'd been attracted to other women since Michelle, but it had been nothing like what he was feeling now. And that unnerved him.

"What?" she asked, noticing him staring at her.

"Your hair is standing on end." Which wasn't untrue. It was, and it was something he could focus on instead of her lips. Or instead of wondering how soft her hair was or how she tasted.

Pull yourself together.

She made a face and shrugged her shoulders. She pulled off her mitts and ran her slender fingers through her hair trying to tame it, but it just seemed to make it worse.

"So you're the governor's son," she said, pulling back her hair and tying it.

"And you're the thorn in my father's side," he remarked.

When Dr. Brown smiled, there was a glint of amusement in her eyes that Henry could only describe as mischievous. "I am, indeed."

He was in trouble.

Big trouble.

Kiera had known that Governor Baker was sending in his son to deal with her today, and she didn't care. That wasn't going to stop her from her mission.

The board of directors and shareholders of Aspen Grace Memorial Hospital were threatening to tear it down and replace it with an elite facility that would cater only to the wealthy who came to ski and frolic in a winter playground, which was all very well, but what about the rest of the people in Aspen?

Those who lived here year-round.

Those who couldn't afford the prices of the wealthy?

Lives were in jeopardy.

And she knew firsthand what a lack of medical care could do, especially when someone couldn't afford it.

Her best friend, Mandy, the only family she had in the world, had been working for a non-profit organization as a nurse. She didn't have insurance, and when an accident left her paralyzed from the waist down all she could afford was an HMO who had botched her surgery. Kiera swore then and there that she would help those who couldn't afford proper medical care. Just like her late mother.

Her mother had been addicted to drugs and unable to get the help she needed, and Kiera didn't really remember her. Just snippets.

The only thing she recalled vividly was fear.

Her father, unable to cope with his own addiction had tried to be there for her, but more often than not she had been alone.

Scared.

Hungry.

Until one day her father had abandoned her in a diner in Colorado Springs.

Kiera swallowed the lump that had formed in her throat. She didn't want to think about her parents.

Or her father.

Or the fact she hoped he'd come back one day.

It wasn't logical.

What *was* logical was saving the hospital. She had to be strong. She couldn't get emotional in front of the governor's son.

She had to be strong. The clinic was all that mattered.

She might be a surgeon in the emergency department, but she gave as much spare time as she could to the free clinic that had started only because she had demanded it. She helped people like her parents and others that couldn't afford health care.

That made her happy.

It kept her busy.

Now, because of greedy bureaucrats, everything was threatened.

Aspen Grace Memorial Hospital was in danger and she was the only person trying to save it. She wasn't unfamiliar with fighting the good fight.

She'd done marches on Washington.

She'd stood up for the rights of people who were marginalized, as much as she could. And she'd taken a minor in social justice at college.

The biggest problem was getting more people on board with saving Aspen Grace Memorial, and it frustrated her. She didn't have the best people skills, and she had a hard time trusting, but she wasn't going to let that stop her.

The chief of surgery was on her side, to an extent, but she was the only one out there in her free time picketing, handing out flyers and attending planning meetings at city hall. Yesterday, she'd been down in the dumps thinking that it wasn't working. Today she felt better now that she was sitting next to Governor Baker's son.

She was getting noticed.

This was the traction she needed.

Do you think all this protesting is wise? Mandy had asked, wheeling herself up to the dining room table where Kiera was working on her sign.

I think so. It's worth it. They want to shut down Aspen Grace Memorial and build some expensive, private hospital. Only the wealthy tourists will be able to afford medical care there.

There are other hospitals, Mandy had stated gently.

With the death of Aspen Grace Memorial comes the death of the free clinic. None of the other hospitals have our free clinic.

Mandy had sighed. *I get that you're doing this for me. You don't have to.*

It's not just for you.

Mandy's expression had softened. *Your mom?*

And your dad. She brushed a tear away. *It's not right. He helped others and no one helped him. He couldn't afford to keep up his practice and pay for his cancer treatments.*

He never did tell me he was so sick, Mandy had said sadly.

He didn't want to burden us.

I would've helped him, Mandy whispered.

So would I.

That had touched Kiera's nerve. It was guilt. Kiera had been off working in Denver. At a hospital that had paid her a lot of money. Growing up poor, growing up in the system, the money had blinded her.

She didn't have so much time for Mandy or Wilfred back then. All that had mattered was work and money.

Mandy had been her only family and vice

versa. Mandy had stayed in Aspen where they grew up, in her late father's home. She had worked as a nurse and was going to start work with Doctors Without Borders. Until the accident. Until the gunshot that had paralyzed her.

If Kiera had been there, she could've had Mandy sent to Denver or to a neurosurgeon who could've done a better job than the HMO did and maybe, just maybe, Mandy would be walking still. If she had been there, she would have paid for better care for Wilfred.

Kiera hadn't been there because she'd been greedy and working in Denver.

And for that, yeah, she felt guilt.

He didn't tell either of us, Mandy had said. *He was stubborn. Don't feel guilty. Although you never listen to me.*

Kiera had smiled and Mandy had taken her hand.

This isn't guilt, Kiera had said quickly. *This is the right thing to do.*

Kiera shook the memory from her head. It made her emotional. Again that pesky lump formed in her throat, and she was quick to swallow it down and get control of her emotions again.

You're strong. Remember that.

Mandy would be impressed that she'd gotten attention from the governor. Even though it actually wasn't Governor Baker himself, it was his son.

Still, it was something.

She'd gotten under the shareholders' skins.

The only thing she hadn't counted on was how handsome Dr. Baker actually was. She had imagined someone different. Like those rich stuffed-shirt bureaucrats she usually dealt with. It had taken her by surprise to see him standing there. Her heart had skipped a beat and her blood had heated.

He made her nervous.

He made her feel naked and exposed, which was unsettling. She didn't like attention. And she had a hard time with feelings of attraction.

She'd suffered enough broken hearts from people who had abandoned her in her life. She usually just locked those feelings away.

It was safer.

She was better off on her own.

Are you?

When Kiera glanced at him, he was looking at her, which sent a shiver, a zing of something down her spine.

He had dark brown eyes that seemed to see right through any kind of facade, and that was unnerving. He had perfectly coifed hair and he was incredibly tall. She pegged him at six foot three, minimum, and she was five foot nine.

The way he looked at her made her sweaty and anxious.

Like when she stood out in a crowd. She always hated that. She preferred to stay out of the limelight. It was how she had learned to survive bouncing from place to place after her mother died and her dad had tried to stay clean and keep a job.

Only he never could.

She tried to blend in, be unseen so he wouldn't get angry at her. And when she was in the system, with other kids, she had remained quiet and hidden. It was easier.

At school and at work, she stayed in the background so people would never use her or hurt her. She knew how to survive.

The one time she had let someone in she'd fallen head over heels in love with Brent.

They had been colleagues and then something more.

She had never before let any man into her heart.

And then he had crushed it.

He had cheated on her and left her.

Abandoned her.

She'd learned her lesson then.

Never again.

Still, the way Dr. Henry Baker looked at her,

like he saw her. He made her tremble with something she had never felt before.

Why are you thinking about how handsome he is? Get control of yourself.

Henry was the kind of guy she used to date before she found out that the men she typically dated didn't really care for the same things she did. The respectable kind of guy that would never fail you or abandon you didn't seem to exist.

She had thought dating men like Dr. Henry Baker, who were educated, would mean they would be interested in the same issues she was. She didn't want a man like her father, who had abandoned her and was only interested in partying.

She'd been sorely mistaken.

Men like Henry couldn't be trusted, either. Brent had taught her that.

When she had left her high-paying job for Aspen, she had expected Brent to follow her, take up the causes she was so passionate about. Instead, he took up with someone else. Someone younger.

Someone who had adored him and hung on to his every word.

It had hurt, and she had become disillusioned with men, but she wasn't going to give up on helping others. Her foster father, the only decent man she had ever known, had taught her that.

Men like Dr. Henry Baker were usually embarrassed by her marches on Washington and her need to be involved in helping those less fortunate, but Kiera was undaunted, so she just stopped dating and focused her time on taking care of Mandy, Mandy's grumpy cat, Sif, and saving lives.

That's what gave her the ultimate fulfillment. *Did it?*

Henry was all wrong for her. He'd be like Brent, not interested in the things she was. Only she couldn't remember having such a strong physical pull toward Brent.

She hated the way her body was reacting being around Henry.

She hated imagining what it would be like to run her hands through the dark brown curls that had just a touch of gray at the sides.

To nibble that strong jawline.

You just met him!

She shook the thoughts away. They'd just lead to trouble and she didn't want trouble.

Yes, you do.

It depended on the trouble and it had been some time since she had felt anything other than numbness. Kiera knew then and there she had to put some distance between her and Henry.

She had to focus.

"So, I'm looking forward to hearing what your father has to say about AGMH and the status of the free clinic. You're obviously here to negotiate."

His eyes narrowed. "No. I'm not here to negotiate."

"What?" she asked, annoyed. "You said that you were. That's why I left the construction site. You wanted to talk to me about terms."

"This isn't some kind of union disagreement. You were alone out there."

"So? If you're not willing to discuss things with me, then you need to stop the car and I'll walk back." She picked up her beanie and jammed it on her head.

He rolled his eyes. "I do want to talk with you, Dr. Brown, but I'm not here to negotiate anything."

She'd heard enough. She was fuming and with the way her cheeks were suddenly hot, she knew they were bright red with anger. That always happened when she got mad. People might mistake it for humiliation, but, really, she was just furious.

"Mike, can you stop the car?" she asked. She knew the governor's personal driver well as he lived in Aspen, and whenever the governor was there, Mike wasn't far behind.

"Sure thing, Dr. Brown." Mike flipped on his turn signal to pull over.

"Mike, don't stop the car," Henry ordered.

"Mike, stop the car." Kiera glared at Henry.

"I have to stop the car, Dr. Baker. You don't live here, and I don't want to be on the bad side of the best surgeon in Aspen," Mike said. "I've got to listen to her."

Henry snorted. "Best surgeon?"

If she was a teapot or some kind of cartoon-like character, Kiera was pretty sure there would be steam shooting out of her ears.

Privileged much? Who did this guy think he was?

The car pulled over and she glared at Dr. Baker. "Thank you for the interesting ride, but I think I'll head back to continue what I was doing."

"No, wait." Henry rolled his eyes and reached out, leaning over her and grabbing her hand to keep it from opening the door. His hand was strong and warm on her cold skin. His body, pressed against her, caused her heart to skip a beat. It caused a rush of something, and this time her cheeks heated for another reason. One she didn't find particularly comfortable.

"Why should I stay here? What's the point? You already told me you weren't interested in listening to me, so why shouldn't I go?"

Henry sighed and scowled. He ran his hand through his perfectly coifed brown curls and sighed again as if in resignation.

"Fine. How about I agree to listen to your reasons for not closing down Aspen Grace Memorial Hospital? Has anyone actually done that? Because from what I understand that's been mostly falling on deaf ears."

Drat.

He was right, of course. No one but the chief of surgery, Mandy and Sif the cat had listened to her, because no one would give her the time of day. She passed out flyers, attended meetings, but nobody seemed to get it.

Now she had a chance.

Dr. Henry Baker was a majority shareholder at AGMH. He was on the board of directors, though usually absent, *and* the governor's son.

She wouldn't get this opportunity again, and even though it seemed no one has been listening she must be making an impact. She was sure of that, because here Dr. Henry Baker was.

No matter how much he scoffed at her and didn't want to negotiate terms with her, he was offering the chance to at least listen to her.

"Okay," she said, pulling her hand back, wanting distance between her and Henry.

Henry moved away from her.

"Good."

"Is it okay to go?" Mike asked, glancing in the rearview mirror.

"Yes," Henry said.

Kiera leaned back against the leather seats. Henry wasn't saying much, but he looked annoyed. She had a feeling he had thought this might be easier. He clearly hadn't been expecting someone like her, but honestly, she hadn't been expecting him either.

"Thank you for taking the time to listen to me, Dr. Baker. I appreciate it."

Henry rolled his eyes again, sighed and nodded curtly. "Well, it's not like I had a choice."

"You could've let me go back to my picketing."

"No, that's not a choice," he said drily. "I just hope this whole thing comes to a quick conclusion. I don't have much time, Dr. Brown."

She pressed her lips together, irritated that he had chided her as if she were a disobedient child.

So infuriatingly arrogant. Sexy, but arrogant.

What was coming over her? She'd never felt this kind of draw to a man before.

Kiera had never really experienced lust. Not even with Brent.

She had been attracted to Brent, but it wasn't like the spark of electricity she was feeling now.

She slid farther away from him, trying to

distance herself physically from the pull of attraction.

"I hope so too, Dr. Baker, because, quite frankly, I don't have time for this, either, and neither do the people whose access to good, quality, affordable medicine you're threatening."

Mike snickered in the front seat and Henry scowled at him.

Kiera sat back against the seat and pulled off her woolen beanie, satisfied that she'd gotten in the last word. This time, at least, because she had a sinking suspicion that this wasn't over.

She imagined she had a fight ahead of her, but it was one she was willing to take on. Even though her boss and Mandy told her it was a battle she wasn't going to win, she was not easily swayed.

Dr. Henry Baker might seem scary and unapproachable to everyone else, but she wasn't everyone else and Aspen Grace Memorial Hospital was her home.

The home that she had to protect.

CHAPTER TWO

KIERA CLEANED HERSELF up in her office, and she thought it might be for the best to let Dr. Baker calm down. He hadn't said much to her since Mike had dropped them off at the hospital

Instead, he had made his way to the boardroom, and she had come straight here. It was good to put some distance between them.

For her own protection.

Plus, they hadn't exactly started off on good terms.

She knew he thought she'd be easy to deal with, when in fact it was the opposite.

Kiera knew exactly what happened when a new, flashier, private practice came into town. She'd heard all the promises before. How the free clinics or other charitable works would be kept open, but inevitably they never were.

They were always the first thing to get the chop.

Always.

And Kiera wasn't going to let that happen to AGMH.

There was a knock at the door, and she turned around to see Dr. Carr hovering in the doorway. He crossed his arms.

"What did you do?" he asked.

"What do you mean what did I do?" she asked innocently.

Dr. Richard Carr was her mentor. He had taught her everything she needed to know about being a surgeon. And when she'd decided to leave Denver and the private hospital she had worked at, Richard had been the first person to offer her a job.

He'd been the only one to encourage her in college because he was the only person she had trusted here. Dr. Carr was kind, and they usually agreed on most things. Except this. She knew they didn't see eye to eye on this.

Richard cocked an eyebrow and looked at her with disbelief as he came into her office and shut the door behind him.

"Dr. Baker is here. You know he's a majority shareholder in the hospital, right? And the son of the head of the board of directors."

"And Governor Baker's son. I get it. I know who he is."

"He has the power to fire you," Richard said, seriously. "So, I'm asking you, what did you do?"

"Nothing. I was protesting at the construction site—like I often do when I have a free moment—and he showed up. He was apparently under the impression that we were going to have a meeting at the hospital."

Richard sighed and crossed his arms. "Were you carrying around one of your signs?"

Kiera bit her lip, her cheeks flushing as she lifted up the sign she had so proudly made. It had been Mandy's idea to add glitter to the dollar-sign eyes.

Richard's eyes widened and he scrubbed a hand over his face. "Lord, have mercy."

"Richard, I wasn't on the actual property. Just the sidewalk around it, and last time I looked this was a free country."

He sighed. "It might be, but you're also a surgeon at this hospital and you might have just screwed yourself over."

"He was prepared to talk to me," she said. "He was willing to hear me out."

Richard was surprised. "He was?"

"Yes. It's why I'm here. I've decided to be professional. No signs, no flyers. No ranting and raving. I can be a professional when I need to be."

A half smile tugged on the corner of Richard's lips. "Yes. I have seen this before."

"What made you think I was in trouble?"

"Dr. Baker is livid. He's pacing in the boardroom. I don't think I've ever seen the man so agitated. Not that I've seen much of him and definitely not since I was hired as chief."

Kiera found that odd. Usually a majority shareholder would take more interest in the hospital, but she knew from an internet search, when she had gotten back to her office, that Dr. Baker worked in a glitzy private clinic in Los Angeles and was something of a playboy.

Had a new, gorgeous, fake woman on his arm every week.

Usually, Hollywood elite.

He was privileged, and Kiera wasn't going to back down because Dr. Baker was throwing a hissy fit. Even if it cost her her job.

The thought scared her because then there would be no one to advocate for the free clinic. There would be no one willing to work it or give it so many hours. What would people do? She couldn't let them down.

It's not your sole responsibility.

Only she'd learned from the best. Mandy's dad, Dr. Wilfred Burke, had given help to those who couldn't afford it.

He'd given her so much.

"I promise to be on my best behavior, Richard."

Richard sighed and walked over to her. "You

know I think of you as a daughter. I've known you since you were a struggling kid in college. Working odd jobs to pay to become a doctor. You were so selfless and so determined. You had it. You have it in you to be a great surgeon, and one of things I love about you is your determination to help others, but you can't do that if you're fired. Kiera, be smart about this. You're fighting for a great cause, but AGMH is falling apart at the seams. You know this and so do I. We're bleeding money, and the last thing the hospital needs is to piss off the majority shareholder."

Kiera sighed. "I know. I promise, Richard."

Richard nodded. "Well, good luck."

"Thanks."

Richard left, and Kiera took a deep breath to calm her nerves.

She could do this.

All she had ever wanted was to be a doctor. She wanted to help the less fortunate. She knew firsthand what it was like not to eat or have a roof over your head. Or to have parents too high to notice you.

Then to spend a year bouncing from group home to group home, waiting for family.

Miserable and scared.

She'd had no real family until the day she

came to a foster home in Aspen. A widower, with a daughter her age.

Then she had had a family.

Then she had belonged.

Dr. Burke had been a good family physician, and he had helped those who couldn't afford care. His selflessness had inspired Kiera to become a surgeon and Mandy to be a nurse.

Mandy was her sister, her best friend.

She owed this to Mandy and to the memory of Dr. Burke. She had to be able to listen to what Dr. Baker had to say to her, just as he had been able to listen to her.

It had been a two-way street.

And they had been able to be professional.

With one last look in the mirror, she straightened her white lab coat, rolled her shoulders back and headed to the boardroom at the end of the hallway.

A ball of dread formed in the pit of her stomach and she felt nervous.

For the first time in a long time.

Don't let him bully you. You got this. You're strong. You've survived worse.

Kiera knocked.

"Come in." His voice was deep and set her on edge.

She opened the door, and at the end of the long, black polished table sat Henry Baker, his hands folded and his eyes staring directly at her. His mouth was pressed into a firm line, and suddenly that ball of dread, turned into a rock.

She felt like she was walking toward her own doom.

Don't let him spook you.

She had faced down scarier people than Dr. Baker. Of course, those other people had been patients, and they hadn't held the fate of her job in their hands.

They also hadn't affected the fate of the hospital.

That was the worrying bit.

Henry was wearing a dark, well-tailored suit, and now that he wasn't huddled down in his flimsy coat, she could clearly see how broad his chest was, and the color brought out the tan from the Californian sun.

Her pulse began to race, her palms sweaty, and she was annoyed that her body was reacting to him again. What was it about him that made her lose control? She didn't date doctors like him for a reason—she'd been burned by Brent. Lulled into thinking he'd cared for her when he was cheating and lying to her. She wasn't making that mistake again.

It was one reason she didn't date anyone. She didn't have time. She didn't trust.

"Shut the door if you will, Dr. Brown." His

voice was deep, serious, and if she had been someone else it definitely would have scared her.

She closed the door and took a seat at the opposite end of the table, not waiting for his invitation, and folded her hands carefully on top of the table. She met his gaze and mustered every ounce of strength she had.

There was a glimmer of amusement in his dark eyes.

"Well, I'm interested in talking terms, Dr. Baker," she said, breaking the tension and silence that he was obviously going for. "I'm hoping we can make this quick. This is my day off, after all."

She knew the moment she said that, she'd made an error. That glimmer dwindled into a dark ember of annoyance.

But if she was going to go down, she was going to go down fighting.

Henry was trying not to see red. As an attending surgeon and a shareholder in other hospitals, he'd had to fire people before. He had reprimanded people. He had respect and he'd gained that respect from the way he handled himself in a boardroom.

He'd taken courses on it at his father's insistence when he was younger. Yet, everything he'd learned didn't seem to have any effect on her.

Why wasn't this working? She was the most infuriating person ever.

Henry could feel his blood pressure rising, and there was a vein in his temple that was beginning to pulsate. He hoped she couldn't see it.

Dr. Kiera Brown unnerved him. She made him feel hot, and also irritated. It was an odd juxtaposition.

She made him want to pull out his hair and also take her in his arms.

She rattled his control.

And he didn't like that one bit.

Now that she was out of her bulky winter wear, professionally dressed and her red hair braided back, he could take it all in. A spattering of freckles across her cute button nose, pink full lips.

Even the cat's-eye glasses she wore complemented her. They were sexy.

She appeared to be professional. As he would expect from a member of staff of one of the hospitals he held shares in, she was a far cry from the woman he'd picked up earlier.

For a moment he forgot who she was.

Until she opened her mouth.

Then his head started to ache.

"I believe I'm the one who called this meeting, Dr. Brown, so I think I should be the one starting off the talk."

She nodded her head in deference. "Fine, but as I said, I have a lot of things to do."

"I thought you had a day off?" he asked.

Her green eyes narrowed. "Yes, but I have to get back to what I was doing, and surprisingly I do have a life outside of this hospital."

"And I don't?" he asked.

She shrugged. "I don't know what you do in your free time. Frankly, that's not my business, just like what I do isn't yours."

He clenched his fist. "It does when your free time activities involve my hospital."

"Your hospital? With all due respect, Dr. Baker, I've never seen you step foot in Aspen Grace Memorial Hospital. Until now, that is."

He rubbed his temples and stood up. "Can we just get on with it? Why are you arguing with everything I say?"

"Are you going to fire me?" she asked bluntly.

Tempting. He kept that thought to himself. He wasn't allowed to fire her although, for her insubordination, he was sorely tempted to do just that. His father had made it clear that Dr. Brown was a valuable and well-liked surgeon both at Aspen Grace Memorial Hospital and in the town of Aspen.

His father didn't want his reelection to be

tainted with firing such a well-known and well-liked surgeon because she was exercising her right to protest.

All his father wanted from Dr. Kiera Brown was to stop the picketing—of her own free will. Not because of the Bakers had persuaded her.

Seduce her for all I care, flitted through his mind.

The prospect had a certain appeal. Kiera was attractive, albeit infuriating.

No, he wouldn't stoop to that level.

Henry really didn't know how he was going to convince her to give up the campaign against the new hospital. And now questioned why he was even here and whether it might have been easier to ignore his father.

Except he couldn't.

He owed his father this and then he'd be free.

He'd no longer be beholden to him.

"No. I'm not going to fire you, Dr. Brown."

"Oh." Her eyes widened and she seemed shocked. She relaxed slightly. "Then why exactly am I here? I mean, you didn't seem quite eager to negotiate terms before."

"And I'm still not." Henry walked down to the end of the table where she sat and leaned over her. He got a whiff of her perfume. It smelled vanilla. It reminded him of a bakeshop.

One that was filled with sweet and sinful delicacies.

Get a hold of yourself.

"Look, tell me what you want. Tell me how I can get you to stop protesting against the new hospital and just do your job. Quietly."

Kiera leaned back and crossed her arms. "I'm doing my job."

"Protesting is not your job." Henry stood up and scrubbed his hand over his face. "Just tell me what I can do, Dr. Brown?"

"Keep the hospital open. It's that simple."

"It's not," he stated.

"Why?"

He sighed. There was no way he was getting into the complicated reason why he was here. He just wanted this dealt with so he could leave this all behind him.

"Henry, are you in here?"

A sense of dread traveled down his spine and curled into the pit of his stomach.

Oh, God. What was she doing here?

"Who's that?" Kiera whispered.

"My mother. Just play along and we'll get her out of here fast."

Kiera looked confused. "Play along? Okay?"

The door opened and his mother sashayed into the boardroom. She was dressed head to toe in designer clothes. It had been a while since he'd seen her. She came to California from time to time, but she never visited him.

He rarely wanted to make time for her. And the feeling was mutual. His mother was not the mothering type.

She only ever wanted to see him when it suited her.

Which was never.

He'd been disappointed enough by her absence in the past.

No one there to comfort him as a child.

She had never been there for any holiday or award he'd won growing up.

He had always been envious of his friends who had mothers who loved and embraced their children. Supported them and cheered them on.

Henry was lucky to get an air-kiss as a token of affection.

His mother was cold and selfish.

"Henry, I thought you'd be in here." She smiled brightly, and Henry walked over to give his mother a quick air-kiss.

"Mother, what're you doing here?" he asked in exasperation.

"I brought someone for you to meet," she whispered loudly. He was pretty sure that Kiera had heard.

"Mother, this is hardly the time and place…"

"Well, then when is the time and place? She's standing outside."

"You brought her here?" he asked under his breath.

"I can go and give you two privacy," Kiera chirped up.

Henry turned around and glared at her.

"I'm sorry, I don't believe we've met," his mother said frostily.

"No. We haven't," Kiera said brightly.

"Do you work here?" his mother asked.

Henry cringed. She wasn't tactful and had no boundaries.

His mother thought she was above everything and everyone else.

"Yes, I do."

His mother nodded and turned back to Henry. "Look, just come outside and meet this lovely woman. She's from a good family."

"Mother, I don't have time for this. Father sent me here to deal with the hospital."

"That can wait." She waved her hand dismissively.

"Mother, I promised Father I'd take care of this, so please let me."

"Honestly, you're acting like this is some kind of hardship. All I'm asking you to do is cooperate. If you choose the right girl and stop with your hedonistic lifestyle it would be so much better for your father's political career."

"That's the only reason you want me to get married?" Henry asked.

His mother's expression softened, which was unusual for her, but only briefly. "It's been eight years since Michelle and all that nastiness after her death—"

"Mother, don't," Henry snapped.

Why did he think anything was going to be different? Why did he think his parents would keep their promise? He should have just blown his father off, and then he wouldn't have to be here. Listening to his parents bring up his mistakes over and over again.

Now he was angry at himself for allowing them to manipulate him.

He wouldn't let his mother embarrass him. He refused to show any kind of emotion. The last time he did his parents had been horrified, so he kept it locked away. Now he was standing here trapped between the rock, which was his mother, and the hard place, Kiera.

Henry took a deep breath to calm his nerves.

How was he going to extricate himself?

Henry glanced back at Kiera, who was smiling, her arms crossed and her eyebrows raised as she watched the whole embarrassing situation unfold. It was mortifying. He was angry with his mother for doing this to him. They wanted him married to the perfect girl for his father's image... Fine, he'd give them that and then some.

"Well?" His mother asked. "Surely you can give me a few moments?"

"No, Mother, I can't. There's no need."

His mother looked confused. "What do you mean there's no need?"

His ears pressurized and his pulse raced. Thundering. He glanced back at Kiera and his vision went a bit blurry. His palms were sweaty.

"There's no need, because I'm engaged already, Mother."

"You're engaged? To whom?" his mother asked, shocked.

He blanked, glanced back at Kiera and took a step toward her.

"Kiera. I'm engaged to Dr. Kiera Brown. We're engaged. It's why I'm here in Colorado. We have to set a date."

CHAPTER THREE

KIERA COULDN'T ANSWER right away because she really didn't know what to say. When Dr. Baker had asked her to play along, she hadn't been expecting to play along with this.

His fiancée? What?

Kiera had to get out of that boardroom. So that's exactly what she did.

There was nothing to say. Let Dr. Baker try to figure out that particular problem on his own.

"Dr. Brown!"

Kiera stopped and waited for Dr. Baker to catch up to her. The last thing she needed was him shouting the ridiculous story he'd just fed his mother all over the hospital.

"Can I help you, darling?" she whispered under her breath.

Henry took her by the arm and led her into an empty exam room. When he shut the door, he let go of her arm and stood with his back to her.

"So when were you going to tell me that we're getting married?" Kiera teased.

"I'm sorry. I panicked." He ran his hand through his hair and turned around. "It seemed like the easy way out."

"The easy way out of what? We're strangers, Dr. Baker, and I think it's safe to say that we don't particularly like each other too much."

Although, honestly, she really didn't know him enough to determine whether she liked him or not. It was what he stood for.

She refused to date or fake marry someone who was concerned about the almighty dollar first and humanity second. She was not going to be with a man like Brent.

She'd seen the pictures in the tabloids of Henry with a different woman each week.

No way.

No more Greedy Guses for her.

Who said he was greedy? You don't know him.

The anxiety rising in her since he'd told his mom they were engaged started to wane.

"Do you always have to be so flippant?" he asked, breaking her chain of thought.

"Sorry," she said, because she did feel for him, even though he had put himself into this situation.

He had also put her into it.

The difference was that she didn't have to take part. She didn't have to go along with his crazy lie.

"So what're you going to tell your mother?"

His eyes widened. "About what?"

"About what we've been talking about. You know, the whole *she's my fiancée* thing? What're you going to tell her now?"

"Nothing."

"Excuse me? What?" She was in shock again. Was she hearing him correctly? She felt like she was stuck in some weird television show where soon someone would jump out at her, tell her she was on camera and throw a pie in her face.

That's how surreal this felt.

"I'm not going to tell her anything different." He crossed his arms in defiance.

"You expect me to do it?"

"Do what?" he asked.

"Tell your mother you lied?"

"No."

She was confused. "What do you mean, no?"

Henry took a deep breath, looking as if he was in pain and rolling his shoulders. "Keep up this pretense and we can talk about what you want. We can talk about the free clinic and Aspen Grace Memorial Hospital."

Her heart skipped a beat. "Are you serious?"

"I can't make any promises, but if you go

along with being my fiancée while I'm here in Aspen, then I will do what I can to make sure your concerns are heard and taken care of."

"So for the next twenty-four hours? You said something about heading back to California?"

"My trip is delayed. My father needs me here and I have a client consult now in Aspen. If, while I'm here, you agree to be my fiancée to keep my parents off my back, I'll see what I can do about your demands."

Something deep down inside of her told her to run, told her not to believe him because she'd been burned before by men like him. Men like her father and Brent. Men who used and abused and never made good on their promise.

Still, this wasn't real and she wouldn't be hurt. She had to remind herself of that.

For whatever reason, he wanted her to pretend to be his fiancée, and though she should say no, the prize was much too great to pass up on. He'd listen to her concerns, and he was willing to work with her. That was the crux of the matter.

And really, what would it cost her? All she had to do was pretend to be his fiancée for the small amount of time he was in Aspen. He wasn't cheating on her, or leaving her locked in some dingy hovel while he scored drugs.

Or leaving her alone at a truck stop diner in the middle of nowhere.

She shuddered as that long-repressed thought slipped into her mind.

She hated that it had come back. She didn't want to feel like the scared, vulnerable girl she used to be.

You still are.

And she shook that thought away.

Kiera was irritated that she had been put in this position.

"Can I think about it?" she asked.

His eyes widened and he looked annoyed. "You want to think about it?"

"Yeah, I do. I mean, an engagement is a big deal."

"You are the most infuriating woman I've ever met!"

"Then I'm going to have to pass." She moved to step past him, but he stood in her way.

"I'm offering you a chance to be heard, have your concerns listened to, and you have to think about it?"

"You're not promising me anything but listening to me. I need something more, and I really need to think about it."

Henry's eyes narrowed. "Fine."

"Thank you."

"Can I take you out to dinner tonight to discuss this further?" he asked.

The invitation caught her off guard. She couldn't remember the last time she had been on a date.

Wait, this wasn't a date.

Only she felt that anxious swirl in the pit of her stomach. Her mouth went dry and her palms were sweaty. All the classic biological signs of attraction.

It was infuriating.

Damn him.

Kiera was tempted to let him sweat it out, but she really did want what he was offering. She wanted her voice heard. She wanted to be listened to.

Lack of medical care for those who couldn't afford it would be devastating.

Mandy's father had taught both of them the power of compassion and medicine. Kiera wanted to help everyone, and the new private hospital would help only a select few.

"Sure. I would like to go out to dinner to discuss this further," she said, finally finding her voice.

Henry relaxed. "Great. Shall I pick you up at seven?"

"Seven is good. I live at two-five-six Green Lane. It's not far from here."

"Green Lane. Got it." He stepped to the side and opened the door for her.

"I look forward to discussing our arrangement further," Kiera said brightly as she moved past him.

He grunted in response.

This was a step in the right direction. Or was it?

She shook that thought away and left Dr. Henry Baker standing in the hall, scowling at her as she left.

Kiera wanted to get back home and fill Mandy in on everything, but as she walked away her pager went off.

There was a large trauma coming in, and they were calling in all available surgeons. Henry ran up beside her.

"What's wrong?" he asked, watching her glance at her pager.

"A trauma. They're calling for all available help to handle it."

"I can lend a hand. I am a surgeon," he offered.

Kiera nodded. "We can use it."

"Lead the way."

When they got down to the emergency room there was a flurry of activity as they tried to make space in the triage for the emergency cases that were expected in. Aspen Grace Memorial Hospital wasn't like other larger hospitals, and they didn't have interns or residents. They had a trauma center and good surgeons, but it meant that every available surgeon was being called in.

For the first time since Henry had arrived, Kiera was thankful he was here.

He was an extra set of hands, and this would give him the perfect opportunity to see that even though AGMH was small, it was mighty.

She got him a pair of scrubs, and they both quickly changed in the locker room.

Kiera handed Henry a yellow trauma gown and a pair of gloves.

Without her having to ask him, Henry tied her gown, and then he turned and she did the same for him, though he had to crouch slightly as he was taller than her. It struck her as odd, but also calming, which was a strange mixture, indeed.

She didn't have to tell him what to do. There was nothing awkward or weird about this.

It was like they both knew, instinctively, what the other needed. Like they had been working together for a long time.

Other than Dr. Carr, her mentor, there wasn't anyone else she worked with so well in the ER. Certainly not a doctor. She relied a lot on the amazing support staff. It was a bit unnerving, and her pulse was racing as she finished tying up his yellow trauma gown. Her cheeks heated. Why was something she did all the time making her feel this way?

All hot and bothered.

Her hands shook as she brushed the nape of his neck.

She finished trying the knot and took a step back.

Trying to regain some control.

She pulled on her mask and slipped on her face shield.

"Do you know what the trauma is?" Henry asked, putting on his own face shield.

"Multi-vehicle collision. Apparently, there was a patch of black ice on one of the mountain passes," another doctor said.

Kiera winced. Black ice was the worst and, on a winding mountain pass road, a recipe for disaster. They stepped outside the ambulance bay doors. The cold wind bit her skin through the thin scrubs, but it wasn't long until they heard the first long, whiny wail of an ambulance siren heading toward them.

Her heart was racing, but it was just the adrenaline. It was her focus. Lives were at risk and she wanted to be here to save them.

The first ambulance stopped and the back

doors opened as the paramedics began to lift the patient down out of the back.

"Patient is a forty-two-year-old female passenger and was ejected through the front window. GCS was three on the scene. BP is sixty over thirty. Suspected head injuries and possible internal bleeding," the paramedic said.

Kiera took over and helped the paramedics wheel the patient into a trauma bay. Henry was on the other side of the gurney. If there were as many injuries as she thought there would be on this patient, she was going to need all the help she could get. To her surprise she didn't need to inform Dr. Baker of what to do, despite his unfamiliarity with Aspen Grace Memorial's trauma room.

He just seemed to know where to go and what to do.

And that was exactly what she needed.

There was no time to explain.

Kiera palpated the abdomen and frowned when she found it was rigid and full.

"Her abdomen is distended. She has internal bleeding. We need to get her into the operating room. Stat."

"Lead the way, Dr. Brown," Henry said.

"Call down and have them prep operating room three," Kiera said to a nurse. "And I'll need a neuro consult."

"Yes, Dr. Brown."

Kiera continued setting up what she needed, to get the patient ready for the operating room. Right now, she and Henry had to get the patient into the operating room and try to stabilize her. She'd have a neurosurgeon in the operating room to monitor, and then once the internal bleeding was under control they could assess the head injury.

While the patient's pupils were still reactive, uncontrolled bleeding could kill her faster.

"You don't need to pull another neurosurgeon in here. I'm a neurosurgeon," Henry said.

"I thought you were a plastic surgeon?" Kiera asked.

"I'm both," Henry stated.

"Okay. Well, that's good to know. Let's get her to the operating room."

Henry nodded and wheeled the gurney out of the trauma room and toward the operating room, which was at the end of the hall from the emergency room. They handed off their patient to the operating room orderlies and made their way into the scrub room, changing out of their yellow trauma gowns and swapping for different scrub caps.

Kiera glanced over at Henry, who was scrubbing in beside her. She noticed how muscular his forearms were. She had a thing for muscular forearms, and peeking out under the sleeve of his scrubs was a tattoo. Her blood heated, and that flutter started in her stomach again.

She had been impressed by the way he had thrown himself into the fray of helping out with the trauma. He just seamlessly fit in. It was sexy as hell watching him work.

And she had a thing about tattoos. She couldn't see all of it, but his looked like the bottom of a tree, roots in particular. It was black and intricate and completely caught her attention. She hadn't taken him for the type of person who had tattoos. Of course, it had been hard to tell what type of person he was under the expensive designer suit.

"What?" Henry asked, noticing that she was staring at him.

"You have a tattoo."

Henry glanced down at his arm. "I do."

"I didn't peg you for the tattoo type."

A half smile tugged at the corner of his mouth. "What kind of person is that then?"

"I don't know." She smiled. "You know, that's the first time you've smiled since you got here. You have a nice smile."

The smile quickly disappeared, and he became serious again, as if he were bothered that she'd noticed he had a nice smile, which he did.

And she quite liked the tattoo, too.

What she didn't like was his moodiness. This hot and cold that he seemed to have. She had just met him, but she didn't know whether she was coming or going with him. One minute he was asking her to pretend to be his fiancée and the next minute he was all closed off and serious. It was driving her crazy.

"I think I should know about your tattoo—we are engaged after all."

Henry sighed and finished scrubbing, shaking the extra water off his hands. "We can talk about this at dinner."

Kiera chuckled to herself as he stepped into the operating room to get on his gloves and gown. She was looking forward to seeing how he worked and whether they would make a good team. She finished scrubbing in and stepped into the operating room.

Henry was operating on the opposite side of the table to Kiera as they repaired the internal damage that was caused by the car accident. The spleen was shredded and there was bleeding around the liver.

Henry kept an eye on the patient's blood pressure, but other than a head laceration, it appeared she was stable. Although, a CT scan would show if there was something that he would need to do.

Right now, they had to get the patient's internal bleeding under control.

As he stood across the table from Dr. Brown, from Kiera, he was impressed with her work. She might be infuriating, but he could see why Dr. Carr wanted to keep Dr. Brown around. She was talented.

So why was she wasting her time protesting the inevitable?

Aspen Grace Memorial Hospital would close.

Why was she wasting her surgical skills in a hospital that was small and falling apart when she could go to any hospital and save lives. Or, she could work in the new place his father and the board were planning to build.

Still, a part of him could see her point.

His father's new hospital wouldn't have an emergency room like this.

It would have trauma services, but only for those with insurance or the funds.

It wouldn't be an open emergency room.

It would only be open for the right price.

He didn't know if the woman they were operating on right now would have those financial means. If it were his father's hospital, she'd be turned away and that thought sobered him. At least, they could provide care like they were supposed to.

It made him resent his father's plans, because no one should be turned away.

He understood what Kiera was fighting for even though this wasn't his fight.

Helping those who couldn't pay their hospital bills was the reason this hospital was losing money. It was like the hospital was bleeding out.

"She lost a lot of blood."

Henry had stood there in disbelief. *"What're you talking about? When I left for Los Angeles she was fine and...she was working up the mountain..."*

Michelle's doctor had nodded slowly. *"The small town she was working in was remote. It was three hours away from the nearest trauma center. They only had a free clinic there and they couldn't handle it. Michelle's insurance wouldn't cover a helicopter ride and there was a storm. There was no way to get to her and we ran out of time."*

"I would've paid for it!" Henry had shouted. *"Why wasn't I contacted? She was my fiancée... she was a surgeon!"*

"I know, Henry. There was no time. If there had been a better hospital..."

"She would've had a chance?"

Sometimes all the money in the world couldn't save lives. So what did it matter?

It hadn't been able to save Michelle.

Aspen Grace Memorial Hospital was falling apart. The new hospital would bring more help to those who needed it.

Billing could take care of those who couldn't pay.

Billing was not his problem. Saving lives was his problem.

"Pressure is dropping," the anesthesiologist said, shaking thoughts of Michelle and the hospital's state of affairs from his mind.

"Having some more fluids. She has another bleeder somewhere," Kiera said.

Henry pulled on the retractor and spotted it. The bleeder on the splenic artery meant that the repair work was over. The spleen was beyond saving. "I think we should do a splenectomy. We have to cauterize the splenic artery."

Kiera cursed under her breath, her brow furrowed, eyes focused on her work. "You're right."

"I know."

Kiera glanced up at him quickly. There was a glint in her green eyes, but he couldn't tell whether it was annoyance or humor. Not with her mask on.

Maybe he'd find out what was going on in her mind if he got to know her better.

And that gave him pause, because he had no plans to get to know her. That's not what he was here for. He was here to do his job, and once that was done he could go back to Los Angeles, where it was sane.

Where it was safe.

He had no idea why that thought had crept into his head.

It was unwelcome.

He didn't want it. He didn't want to have that kind of thought.

They finished with the splenectomy and Henry scrubbed out next to Kiera. An awkward tension settled between them.

"So much for your day off," he said, trying to make conversation.

Silence had never bothered him before, but now he was uncomfortable and making small talk.

Which he found infuriating.

Brutally and blindingly infuriating.

"That's okay," Kiera sighed. "I love my job."

"You know, it's a bit weird without interns and residents here."

"Why?" she asked.

"You're a good surgeon. You should be teaching others."

Pink tinged her cheeks. "Well, there's no teaching program set up here."

"There should be. There could be if this new hospital was built."

Her eyes narrowed and her spine straightened. "Maybe if the money for the new hospital was put into Aspen Grace Memorial Hospital, then it could expand and build a teaching program."

"There's no reason to build on here," Henry said, his voice rising. "The new land…"

Kiera held up her hand. "Look, we can talk about this at dinner. I don't want to argue in the operating room."

"You still want to have dinner with me?" he asked, shocked. He had thought for sure that she would change her mind.

For one fraction of a second, he began to doubt his rash plan to tell his mother he was engaged to Kiera, and his brain was trying to formulate how to get out of it.

Kiera smiled, sending a chill down his spine. As if this was far from over.

"Of course," she said sweetly. "We are engaged and have a lot of things to discuss."

"That we do," he said drily.

Kiera finished scrubbing out. "It'll be okay."

He cocked an eyebrow and smiled. "Somehow I don't think that it will."

She chuckled and dried her hands. "I'll see you at seven?"

Henry nodded, still a bit dumbfounded by everything that had happened since he'd gotten off the plane. He was missing Los Angeles, he was missing the sun. He was missing his work. No one bugged him there.

He wasn't annoyed when he was doing what he loved, when he was in his own space, in his own practice.

Kiera left and he finished scrubbing out.

It would have been easier to ignore his father and stay in his blissful bubble in Los Angeles.

Your blissful, lonely bubble.

Only he had almost ruined his life, his practice, everything when Michelle died.

His father had saved him and never let him forget it.

Henry sighed and grabbed paper towels to dry his hands. He quickly dried his hands and tossed the paper towels in the garbage. He was dreading tonight for a number of reasons.

Mostly though, he was dreading being alone with Kiera.

She drove him crazy, but she was feisty, beautiful and talented, and that was always a dangerous combination for him.

She was exactly the type of woman he liked.

Women like Kiera excited him.

They made him feel alive and he hadn't felt like that in a long time. It was a scary feeling. Kiera was the type of woman he had avoided for the last eight years because it was too dangerous for him.

He wasn't going to be hurt again.

He wasn't going to feel that pain, that gut-wrenching loneliness and the hole that Michelle's death had left in his heart.

So Kiera was dangerous for him.

She threatened his heart.

CHAPTER FOUR

KIERA OPENED THE door to the home she shared with Mandy. Though it was technically Mandy's home, Kiera had lived there since she was a young girl, when Dr. Burke had taken her in as his foster daughter.

"Kiera?" Mandy called out from the kitchen.

"Yeah. I'm home." Kiera shut the door as Mandy wheeled herself in from the kitchen.

"You were gone longer than I thought," Mandy said. "I was getting worried. There was an accident on the road, some black ice."

"I know." Kiera hung her coat up. "I got called into the operating room. I was helping with the trauma cases."

"Well, that explains it." Mandy relaxed, but for a brief moment Kiera could see an expression she knew so well. It was a mixture of relief and envy. Mandy missed her work. She missed helping others, taking care of the injured. It had always been Mandy's dream, but after the ac-

cident and her lengthy recuperation, her career
had been ruined.

She could still be living out her dream.

And what about your dreams?

Kiera shook that thought away. She was living her dream—she was saving lives. She had
had other dreams, like having a family. That
felt frivolous now. Mandy and her father had
taken care of her when she was young, lost and
had no hope.

They had made her feel safe. They had made
her feel loved.

They had given her a chance.

This was where she was supposed to be, so
all those other dreams were just that. They were
dreams. She couldn't trust anyone else with her
heart enough to have that secret fantasy of marriage and babies.

The one time she had thought of having all
that had been when she was with Brent. When
Mandy had still been working and Dr. Burke
was still alive. When her life had been perfect.
Or she had thought it was. Everything fell apart
soon after that.

Brent cheated on her. Mandy was shot, and
Dr. Burke died with a ton of bills.

Mandy and AGMH were her life, her family now.

"Sorry I didn't call."

Mandy shrugged. "No worries, but I'm glad you weren't one of the injured. The roads out there were wicked."

"They're not too bad now. The salters have been out." Kiera sighed and made her way to the living room, sitting down on the sofa and leaning back.

There was a meow and an orange tabby jumped up beside her. Sif was Mandy's orange tabby but mixed with something. She had the grumpiest face. All smushed and grumpy like. Kiera always wondered what Sif was mixed with.

The devil most likely, but today was an angel.

That was something. She had dealt with one too many grumpy souls today.

At least Mandy's cat liked her today.

"So, you got called in from your day off?" Mandy asked, coming into the living room.

"I did, but I got pulled off the protest *long* before the accident happened."

Mandy cocked an eyebrow. "How come?"

"Don't sound so amazed."

"I am amazed. You're pretty focused, even somewhat crazed, when you're out there."

Kiera chuckled. "Thanks."

"It's the truth," Mandy teased. "On your days off you should be enjoying yourself. Living life."

"I am enjoying myself."

Mandy stared at her skeptically. "Uh-huh. Sure. So, who managed to tear you away from your mega fun day of protesting?"

Kiera sighed. "The governor's son and the majority shareholder."

Mandy's eyes widened. "Wow. They sent in the big guns, huh?"

"You know who I'm talking about?"

"I do. Dr. Henry Baker is one of the foremost neuro and plastic/ENT surgeons on the West Coast. He has shares in many hospitals, not all of them part of his father's vast empire."

"Vast empire?"

"The Bakers own a lot of Colorado. A lot."

"No wonder he's so arrogant," Kiera mumbled. "He's privileged."

Mandy chuckled. "You could say that, but he doesn't seem to run in the same circles as his parents. He rarely comes to Colorado. You must have made some kind of impression on the Bakers if they brought in Henry to deal with you."

"Well, I feel honored, I guess." Kiera paused. She wanted to tell Mandy about the deal she and Henry had made, but also she didn't. It was clear that Henry was privileged—she knew that— but now she felt guilty for agreeing to Henry's crazy plot.

So he didn't want to be harassed by his parents for not getting married and continuing on the family dynasty.

That wasn't her problem.

Still, the temptation of what he was offering was hard to pass up. To save the free clinic, to save the hospital, the hospital she loved.

It was just a lie.

"What," Mandy asked, as if reading her thoughts.

"What?" Kiera's cheeks heated.

"There's something you're not telling me. I can read you like a book, Kiera. What happened today?"

"I was told to stop picketing." Which wasn't a complete lie, she had been.

"Did you get fired?" Mandy asked, worried.

"No. I didn't get fired. They wouldn't fire me for exercising my free will."

"Then what?"

"I'm going out to dinner in an hour with Dr. Baker."

Mandy's eyes widened and she smiled. "You're going on a date with the enemy?"

"I know," Kiera said drily.

"That's kind of fun," Mandy teased. "He's kind of handsome. Or at least he was the last time I saw him."

"He still is that." Her blood heated, and she didn't like that she was reacting to Henry. Sure, he was good-looking, but she'd met other good-looking men before and didn't know what it was about him that got under her skin so much.

What was different about him?

Why did he make her feel this way?

There was something about him that unnerved her. Like he could see through all her protective layers. He looked at her with a hunger that she was sure was reflected in her own eyes.

And she couldn't recall ever lusting for or being so attracted to someone like this.

What was also frustrating was he drove her absolutely crazy.

"So I guess I didn't need to save you spaghetti." Mandy headed back to the kitchen. The whole lower level of the older cottage-style home was open concept so that Mandy could get around easily.

It was accessible. Mandy's bedroom and bathroom were now in what used to be her father's office when he had his practice out of his home.

Kiera had the top floor, where there was a washroom and a large gabled room that she used to share with Mandy when they were younger.

Before Mandy's father died.

Before the accident.

When life had been simpler.

And Sif, the cat, just ruled the entire house.

"What're you going to wear?" Mandy asked from the kitchen.

"What do you mean what am I going to wear?"

"You can't wear what you're wearing. You're going out with a Baker," Mandy teased.

"So?" Kiera asked, puzzled.

"He's probably going to take you to one of the private restaurants in the resorts. One of those fancy restaurants up near the ski lifts or something."

"Ugh, I hope not."

"Come on, live a little. You said so yourself, you thought he was handsome."

"Why are you so invested in this?" Kiera asked.

"Because you never go out or have fun. You deserve to have fun. Sexy fun, even?" The last bit was said with hope.

"I can't stand him. He's trying to shut down my program. He's trying to shut down my hospital."

Mandy shot her a funny look. "So? Live a little. If I were you…"

"You're going to try to guilt me into dressing up, aren't you?"

Mandy smiled deviously. "Maybe. Is it working?"

"No." Kiera sighed. "Fine, I'll change."

"Do your makeup and hair. Wear heels."

"What is with you? Since when did you become my fairy godmother?"

"Oh, I quite like that title," Mandy teased as she scooped a large spoonful of spaghetti out of the pot and plopped it into a plastic container, making a squelching sound. "Besides, with you out of the house maybe Derek will come over."

"Derek? Our neighbor Derek?" Kiera asked, surprised.

Mandy smiled and a blush tinged her cheek. "He comes over from time to time when you're on a long shift."

"Oh. That's great." Kiera was surprised by that. Not that Mandy couldn't date or anything, but she had never seemed to be interested in doing so since the accident. She had never seemed to want to. All she had wanted to do was hang around with Kiera. Which was fine.

She wanted to take care of Mandy.

You deserve a life, too.

"When is he picking you up again?" Mandy asked, looking at the clock.

"Seven."

"You have an hour. You'd better get started. Dazzle him."

Kiera laughed, rolled her eyes and got up off the couch. Sif stared at her in disgust for leaving her and not continuing to pet her. Kiera was tired, and really all she wanted to do was curl up and go to sleep.

That was her life. Work, saving the hospital and sleep.

Kind of pathetic.

She shook that thought away and headed upstairs. She walked into her room and opened her closet. It was kind of bare. And she could barely remember the last time she had gone on a date.

And then it came to her.

Brent.

He used to wine and dine her. The first man to do so. She thought he'd been the one. Her Prince Charming.

Boy, was she wrong.

When she'd told him her plans for Aspen, he'd told her his plans for someone else. Even then, she rarely dressed up for him.

"I don't have anything to wear," she shouted down the stairs. "Unless you let me go to dinner in scrubs?"

"No!" Mandy shouted. "You're not going to dinner in scrubs, or jeans or any kind of trouser. You're going to wear pantyhose, heels, makeup, and I'm going to do your hair. I'm going to live vicariously through you!"

Kiera smiled to herself. "Fine."

"I have a dress you can borrow. Have your

shower, and then come down to my room and I'll help get you ready."

"Okay."

There was no point in arguing. She was invested in this project now.

Kiera had a quick shower and made her way back downstairs to Mandy's room. Mandy had already pulled out a dress and laid it on the bed with a pair of heels. She was taken back by the unfamiliar garment. It was the most beautiful color of jade she'd ever seen.

It was silk and it shimmered in the light. It was a halter-style silk dress that would come just below her knees and looked formfitting, which made her nervous.

She didn't usually wear clothes like this.

Clothes like this exposed her, and she was too good at keeping herself hidden. She didn't like attention drawn to her unless she was protesting something worth fighting for. Any extra layer protected her. This dress left nothing to the imagination.

There was no hiding in this dress.

Hidden was safe, and she wanted that safety tonight.

It's why she liked scrubs. They weren't formfitting—everyone wore them. She blended in when she was at the hospital.

Funny for someone protesting all the time.

She shook that thought from her head. That was different.

This dress made her nervous. It was then she saw Henry's eyes in her mind. That gaze he gave her. The one that made her weak in the knees and flustered.

"Where did you get that?" Kiera asked, running her hand over the silken fabric.

"Well, it was actually for your birthday next month, but since you're going on a hot date, I thought you might like it now."

"You bought it for my birthday?" Kiera asked softly.

"I did." Mandy smiled sweetly. "You never go out, you never have fun and I saw it in the shop. It was made for you, and I wanted you to have it. I was going to take you out to one of those fancy places in town for your birthday anyways, but now you're going somewhere probably even more glamorous than where I was going to take you. No buts, you need to wear this."

Kiera sat down on Mandy's bed and threw her arms around her. "You're really the best friend a girl could ask for."

"I know. Also, you're damp, so you're wrecking my sweater and I have a date tonight, too."

Kiera laughed, trying to force back the tears that were threatening to spill. "Thank you."

"Go get dressed in my bathroom. I want to see this on you. That's the least you could do."

"I thought dressing up and letting you do my makeup was the least you could do?"

"Whatever, just do it," Mandy said.

"Fine." Kiera picked up the dress and went into Mandy's bathroom. She hung the dress on the back of the door and stared at it for a few minutes. She'd never had anything quite this nice before.

This was the kind of dress she'd always dreamed about when she was a young girl.

Daddy, can I have a dress? she'd asked, looking in the window of a store that had a pink frilly dress. She'd been able to see other girls trying it on with their mothers.

No, her father had snapped, his voice shaking, and she knew he was coming down off his high. *You're ungrateful.*

I'm not, Kiera had whispered.

You are, her father had yelled.

Tears had stung her eyes and she'd wiped them away.

And now here she was, holding a dream dress.

A lump formed in her throat.

Green was always her color.

She rarely wore it, though, because people noticed her when she wore green. And she didn't like to be noticed that way.

When her dad had been on a bender or partying with his dealers and the unsavory crowd, it had been good to remain hidden.

The same thing in the foster homes.

It had been better to stay out of sight.

Was it?

And even though she didn't like to be seen, she got a secret thrill knowing Henry would see her in this dress.

Her palms were sweaty as she touched the dress and as she thought of her upcoming date. What was she doing? This wasn't smart. This was dangerous.

Henry decided to drive himself.

The roads were better, and he really didn't need Mike's sarcastic remarks tonight or him knowing about the deal with Dr. Brown. If Mike knew, he would tell his father and the whole plan would be blown.

The point of this was to get his parents off his back about getting married. And to annoy his father.

He knew that his father wanted to run for something more than governor one day, and having a single son who dated Hollywood starlets and was constantly in the gossip magazines didn't exactly look good for his father's political career. Henry's lifestyle didn't mesh with his father's political agenda.

Which was fine by him.

As soon as this was all dealt with his father would be off his back and he would have to deal with AGMH or Colorado again.

Would his father really release him from his debt?

That was something he hadn't worked out yet. He didn't want to think that far ahead, although his brain was wired to do so.

Tonight he would deal with the here and now.

He'd worry about the details later, which was unlike him and why he didn't usually go into this kind of situation blindly. The more he thought about it, the more agitated he got. His palms were sweaty as he gripped the steering wheel and his jaw ached from grinding his teeth together.

You need to focus, Henry.

He was used to being alone. He preferred it. He was used to quiet.

He had to calm down or he'd never get through dinner.

He was still in shock that he had invited Kiera out.

Why? Had he forgotten she was his fiancée? Henry smiled at that. What was he getting so worked up about? Maybe because he couldn't stop thinking about her?

In fact, he couldn't get her out of his head. After working with her in surgery, he could think of nothing else.

He couldn't stop thinking about her slender hands holding the scalpel, the way she operated with such grace and care. It had been a long time since he'd enjoyed operating with a surgeon he didn't know well.

Usually, he liked to work alone. Only then did he have control and control meant that he didn't have to rely on anyone else.

Which meant he wouldn't be disappointed or hurt.

Or angry because he'd been let down.

His practice focused mostly on plastics and ear nose and throat. That's why people in Los Angeles came to see him, because of his surgical prowess. His perfection. He didn't let his patients down.

It's why they paid him a lot of money.

Money that he didn't know what to do with other than invest it in hospitals.

He'd forgotten how much he liked working in trauma and on the general surgery aspect. The rush of saving a life rather than making someone beautiful.

He did save lives, though.

There were times he did surgeries to repair the effects of cancer. To help with the mental health and well-being of others, but in Los Angeles they were few and far between.

He'd forgotten how satisfying it was to save a life. To really get in there and help a patient out of danger.

That was what Michelle had liked most about medicine. That's why she had worked with first responders and flown into remote places—to save lives when time really was the essence. Michelle had helped so many people, but in the end…no one could save her.

No one had been there for her.

A lump formed in his throat and he shook the fleeting thoughts from his mind as he pulled up in front of Dr. Brown's house. Then it struck him that he remembered this place from when he was a young boy.

This used to be a doctor's office. A family practitioner.

Dr. Burke.

Dr. Burke had looked after Henry when he had broken his leg skiing. Henry had fond memories of the kind, widowed doctor and his two daughters. Though he had never talked to them, he remembered vividly them playing in the front yard, building snowmen.

He was seventeen and they had to have been

about eight or nine years old. He had been jealous because they had looked like they were having fun and Henry had never been allowed as a kid to build a snowman or frolic like that in public.

Everything about his childhood had been regimented by his father's political career and his growing up had taken place in boarding schools and with nannies.

So he had envied Dr. Burke's daughters playing in the snow. So happy. One had brown hair, but it was the redheaded girl who had caught his attention because she was sitting up in a tree and pelting neighborhood boys with snowballs. Her red hair had been so bright against her tattered snowsuit.

It had caught his eye.

He'd laughed. And hoped that if he ever had kids, he'd give them a childhood like this—the one he hadn't got to have—and he would teach any daughter of his to defend herself against boys, too. To stick up for herself.

It's why he had always liked strong-willed women.

It then hit him who that redheaded hellion kid was.

No. It couldn't be. Perhaps she just lived in Dr. Burke's old place. Dr. Burke had died several years ago.

His pulse was racing as he stared up at the house again. He got out of the car and made his way up a wheelchair ramp that hadn't been there before. That's when he started to calm down. There had been no wheelchair ramp when Dr. Burke had been practicing.

Also, Kiera's name was Brown. Not Burke.

Henry took a deep breath and knocked on the door.

The door opened and he looked down shocked to see Mandy Burke, in a wheelchair.

"You must be Henry Baker? It's been a long time," Mandy said brightly. "I haven't seen you around these parts since you were a teenager."

"Mandy? Dr. Burke's daughter?"

Mandy smiled. "One and the same. Come on in."

"I thought this was Dr. Brown's house?" he asked, confused, stepping in and closing the door behind him.

"It is. She lives here. We grew up together."

"You grew up together? In this house?"

"Yes." Mandy cocked her head to one side. "You okay?"

"Just confused. Does your sister still live here?"

"Sister?" Mandy asked, confused. "I don't have a sister. All I have is Kiera."

His stomach sank like a rock as it hit him

that the little girl he had thought so funny for taking on the neighborhood boys so long ago, the one with the red braids sitting up in that big tree, was Kiera.

It hit too close for comfort.

"I'll let Kiera know you're here," Mandy said. "Why don't you have a seat?"

"Okay." Henry sat down, a bit dazed, on the nearby couch, only to be met with a hiss and howl as a big orange cat jumped up and then took off like a shot as Mandy texted something on her phone.

"Don't mind Sif," Mandy said as she looked up from her phone. "She really hates strangers. Especially men."

"Great."

Sort of a fitting cat for Kiera.

It was then that Kiera came down the stairs. The first thing that he saw were her legs. Long, shapely legs that made him feel hot and bothered.

That was usually the first thing he noticed on a woman.

He couldn't help but think of those legs wrapped around him or running his hands over them.

Remember who this is. This is Dr. Brown, who you've made a deal with.

Only, he really didn't care.

She came down the rest of the stairs and he was stunned by her.

She took his breath away.

This wasn't the same woman he'd met all bundled up and marching with a sign.

But it was.

The color green suited her perfectly.

It brought out the green of her eyes, the coral color of her lips. And her eyes seemed to sparkle and dazzle in the light. Her red hair cascaded down over her bare shoulders, and he fought back the urge to run his hands through her hair.

He was absolutely speechless.

There was a pink blush to her cheeks as their gazes locked.

"I hope I'm not overdressed," she said, clearing her throat.

"You're not," he said, hoping that his voice didn't crack. "You look lovely."

The pink blush deepened. "Thank you."

"Shall we go?" he asked.

"Sure." She bent over and Mandy whispered something to her. There was a sparkle in Kiera's eye as she glanced back at him, a small smile on her face.

It made his heart skip a beat.

That look held some kind of promise, and he was fighting back the urge to find out what it would be like to kiss her. To have her smile for a different reason.

He wanted to know her secrets.

Focus.

Kiera grabbed her coat and he took it from her, helping her put it on. His fingers brushed the soft skin of her shoulders. He wanted to touch her more and he kicked himself for wanting that.

That's not why he was here.

This was supposed to be a business dinner.

He held open the door for her and she led the way down the ramp. He opened the door to his car and she carefully sat down, flashing him a bit more leg, which sent another zing of electricity through his body.

Damn. This was going to be harder than he'd thought.

What had he gotten himself into?

He walked around the car and got into the driver's seat, trying to ignore that she was sitting right beside him. That they were alone.

Together.

Two strangers.

"No Mike tonight?" Kiera asked.

"No. I thought it should be just the two of us. You look very nice tonight, Dr. Brown."

"I think we'd better be on a first-name basis, don't you agree?" she asked.

"You're right."

"Although, I will admit it feels weird to call you Henry. We don't know each other."

He smiled as he drove away from the house. "I agree. Although, I do remember you now."

"What?"

"When I was a teenager Dr. Burke treated my broken leg. Most of his home, back then, had been a little clinic of sorts. My father liked Dr. Burke and had the housekeeper take me there. When I was there, I remember his two daughters playing in the snow. You were in a tree, throwing snowballs at a bunch of neighborhood boys."

She smiled. "Those boys were jerks."

He laughed. "I didn't know you were Dr. Burke's daughter."

"I'm not. Not really. I was adopted when I was ten. He's not my biological father."

"But he raised you."

"Yes." She smiled.

"Biology doesn't dictate family." And that was true. He had biological parents, but he didn't feel any real connection to them compared to some of the people they had hired to take care of them. He had had a teacher in medical school who took him under his wing and he felt more for that man than he did his own father.

His parents were always leaving him.

They hadn't raised him.

Others did.

He was more than ready to get this job over and done with so he could forget about his parents.

About his past.

He could move on.

Can you?

She smiled. "I always thought that, too."

"I was sorry to hear that he died. I was in California." He cleared his throat. "When did Mandy. I mean when…"

"She had an accident about eight years ago. Just after her father died," Kiera said, softly. "She had just graduated from nursing college, had no insurance and a horrible HMO who botched a very simple lumbar fusion. It paralyzed her."

"I'm sorry to hear that."

Kiera sighed. "I wasn't there. I should have been. Forget I said that."

"Said what?" He glanced at her briefly and she smiled at him.

"So where are we going tonight?"

"My parents are having a dinner. I was going to take you to a lovely, private restaurant, but my mother got word that we were going out and insisted we stop in for one of her charity dinners."

"What?" Kiera asked, clearly uncomfortable. "We are supposed to talk negotiation."

"Think of this as that. We do have to prove that you're my fiancée."

"I'm not able to handle the rich and famous of Aspen, although most of them don't even live here." Her voice rose and she was obviously upset. "We don't come from the same world."

"I believe we're both from Earth."

She chuckled. "Okay. Fine."

"We just have to make an appearance. Have a drink, dinner and then I'll take you home. Maybe if your cat doesn't attack me, we can talk about it at your place."

"My cat?" she asked.

"I sat on your cat," he said, annoyed.

She laughed. "Right, that's what Mandy said. You sent Sif into a tizzy."

"Sif?"

"Yes, but Sif isn't my cat. She's Mandy's cat. Sif does claim me."

"I thought it must be yours, seeing how it hated me and all," he teased, winking.

Kiera laughed. "No. Not my cat, but I will have to give her a treat later."

Henry rolled his eyes. "So, do we have a deal?"

"I'm still not comfortable with this."

"Well, think about it—most of the people at this fund-raiser tonight are people who have power. Power to give money to hospitals, money to give to keep certain free clinics open or possibly stop hospitals from closing."

He looked at her again and could see the wheels were turning.

"Why are you taking me there? I thought your father wanted to stop me protesting?"

"And I have stopped that. He doesn't want you protesting in public, but I can't stop you from talking privately to investors and those who have money and political sway, can I? I mean, I might be your fiancée, but I'm not in control of you."

Kiera grinned and he couldn't help smiling. "I never thought I would say this, Dr. Brown, but right now you're my favorite person and I like the way you think."

CHAPTER FIVE

HENRY HAD LOST track of Kiera. Once he had told her she had free rein to talk to anyone she wanted at the fundraiser—provided she keep up the pretense of being his fiancée—she had taken off, and he had watched her as she worked a room.

She might like to hide, but when it came to Aspen Grace Memorial Hospital and that free clinic she was so determined to save, she came out of her shell instantly.

It was like all these people his parents were schmoozing were the neighborhood boys and she was in that tree just pelting them with snowballs.

He chuckled to himself as he took a sip of his champagne.

Also, he liked watching her from a distance. Admiring her. She lit up the room And in that dress, he couldn't tear his eyes off her. At least while she was schmoozing he couldn't be tempted to take her in his arms, because that's what he'd been struggling with all night as he watched her. She really was the most beautiful thing he'd seen in a long time.

He hated the fact that he was so attracted to her.

He had dated other women, beautiful women, but this was different. There was something about Kiera that drew him in. She was infuriating, smart, sexy.

She made his blood heat with lust, his pulse race with need.

She wasn't as shallow as the women he usually dated. She didn't want to use him. He was using her.

And he felt bad about that.

He was using her because being engaged to her would annoy his father the most. He might have to do this last thing for his father, but he was going to get some enjoyment out of it.

And that was picking someone who would irritate his father.

But that wasn't the only reason he had chosen her.

She was like a breath of fresh air.

She's not actually yours.

He had to keep reminding himself of that.

Henry tore his gaze away from Kiera, wandered past the crowds and headed toward a more quiet section of his parents' party. To a large floor-to-ceiling window that overlooked the mountains and the trees. He couldn't see the trees in darkness, but he could see the mountain lit up and people skiing.

Not long ago they had been saving someone's life. The road had been covered in black ice while the snow fell.

Now, it was like none of that had happened. It scared him how fast life moved on, that it carried on like everything was okay.

"There you are."

He turned when he heard Kiera approach. His pulse raced when he saw her. His gaze raked over her curves, because that dress didn't hide a thing and he liked what he saw.

"I thought you'd ditched me," she said.

"No. Parties like this aren't my jam. So I stay on the sidelines."

She cocked her head to one side. "You're always at Hollywood parties."

"Not by choice," he murmured. "Have you heard about the status of the patient we worked on? You didn't mention it when I picked you up."

"I have. She's stable and is expected to make a full recovery. That accident was bad, but it could've been worse. There were no fatalities."

"Good."

"Is something wrong?" Kiera asked.

"Nothing. I just hate these kind of parties."

"So why do you attend them then?" she asked.

He thought about it. "I don't know."

Although he did. In this instance it was a condition of his bail from his parents. These parties reminded him of his loneliness.

His parents preferred these types of gatherings to being with him.

"You want to go?"

He cocked an eyebrow. "Are you done working the crowd?"

"I am. See, the thing is, these parties aren't my thing either, but I don't look a gift opportunity in the mouth. I'm ready to leave, and hopefully we can finish our conversation. You know, the real reason you asked me out."

"I would like that." He set his champagne flute down on a table and held out his arm.

"I forgot to tell you something," she said, taking his arm.

"Oh?"

"You look really good in that tuxedo."

He chuckled, secretly pleased. "I'll take the compliment, Dr. Brown. I haven't had many from you since I arrived this morning."

Kiera was smiling, which he interpreted as a good sign.

He was more than ready to leave. And he

wouldn't mind continuing their date in a more private location.

This is just a business arrangement. This is not real.

Suddenly he wished it was because he wanted her.

"Henry!"

He froze and grumbled as he heard his mother call him. He turned around, and his mother made her way through the crush of people.

"You two are leaving?" his mother asked, exasperated.

"We are, Mother. Kiera has work tomorrow and I have work to do for Father. Unless you have forgotten? We made an appearance like you requested," Henry said stiffly. He was annoyed his mother had interrupted his plans to escape unseen.

He didn't want her intruding on this. He was glad he didn't have to speak to his father, who was too busy wooing potential donors for his political career.

So, what else was new?

"Oh. Well, very well." His mother looked disappointed. "Do be careful getting home. I heard the roads up the mountain have gotten bad."

"We will." He gave his mother a perfunctory kiss on the cheek.

Henry's parents hadn't interacted with Kiera

anyway. His mother had barely acknowledged her, but they had tolerated her here because she was a doctor and she was his fiancée. His parents saw Kiera as a political tool.

She looked good on paper.

Was he doing the same? His stomach knotted as that thought crossed his mind. He didn't like it, but it was the truth. He was using her. Kiera didn't know about his past or that he was here in Aspen because he owed his father.

And she didn't need to know.

This wasn't real.

It would be over soon enough.

Henry instinctively put his hand on the small of Kiera's back as he led her away from his mother, from his parents so-called friends.

He just wanted to leave. They got their coats and waited outside for the car to be brought around. Only once they were in the car and driving away from his parents' mountain lodge did he finally break the silence.

"I'm sorry for dragging you to that."

"It was fine," she said.

"You don't have to be nice about it." He glanced over at her.

She chuckled. "It really was okay. I did get to talk to a lot of powerful people and let them know what's happening with Aspen Grace Memorial Hospital."

"You think you swayed them?" he asked.

"I'm not sure whether I did or not, but at least I got to talk to them."

He was impressed with her. Her strength and the way she didn't seem bothered by it all. Why couldn't she have been this easy dealing with him earlier in the day?

"Also," she said. "I found they were easier to talk to when I mentioned that I was your fiancée. That they were talking to the future Mrs. Baker."

He smiled. "Don't you mean Dr. Baker?"

"Some of them weren't too open to the idea of calling me doctor, but that's sort of old-school. I'm the pretty wife," she teased, and he laughed with her.

"Well, that's not a lie."

"What's not?"

"The pretty part." And the moment he said it, he regretted it. It had slipped out. Not that he regretted saying she was pretty—that wasn't it at all—but that he had let her know, had admitted he found her attractive.

And he did find her attractive.

It's just that he couldn't have her. He didn't want to open his heart again. The risk of pain was too much for him to bear and the guilt of moving on with someone like Kiera, someone who reminded him of Michelle in spirit, was a big no-no.

That's why he dated the women he did.

He didn't date women who reminded him of Michelle.

Yet, here he was with Kiera.

They weren't dating, but he was pretending to be engaged to her.

"Thanks," she said, her voice rising a bit, and he knew that she was uncomfortable with his compliment.

An uneasy tension fell between them again. The only sound was his wiper blades, brushing the snow off his windshield. It made a horrible screeching sound, which just added an extra layer of tension.

"So, we haven't really gotten to talking about terms," she said, finally breaking the silence.

"Terms?"

"Yes. What will I get, Dr. Baker? Or more importantly what will you give to Aspen Grace Memorial Hospital?"

Kiera had not been expecting to be taken to a function like that. At first, she had been completely unsure about the idea because she was already uncomfortable wearing the dress, but then it had worked out well.

She wasn't sure if what she said was getting

through to anyone at the party, but at least she was talking. At least she was getting her viewpoint across to those in power.

Talking about the hospital was easy.

What unnerved her was the way Henry had looked at her. It had given her a thrill. It had made her pulse quicken, her blood heat, and when he had put his hand on the small of her back as they were leaving, it had felt right.

It had made her want him.

And she didn't like that one bit. She didn't have time for this.

She wasn't going to be hurt again.

By anyone.

She didn't want him to talk about how pretty she was, even though she enjoyed it. She wanted to talk about how handsome he was in his tuxedo because he really did look good. The tuxedo was well tailored and fit his body like a glove.

She couldn't help admiring the way he looked.

He looked good enough to eat.

Her cheeks heated as the thought crept into her mind. She couldn't think that way. She had to focus, and focusing on the hospital would do just that.

"What will I give to Aspen Grace Memorial Hospital?"

"Yes. I mean that was part of the deal, wasn't it? I pretend to be your fiancée to get your parents off your back, and you help me and my hospital. You have the power. You're a majority shareholder, you could convince the others to change plans."

"Changing plans isn't that easy," he said, and she could hear the exasperation in his voice. "Land has been bought."

"That free clinic gives quality medicine to those who won't be able to afford the private hospital. Surgeons donate their time there."

Henry sighed. "It's very noble."

"And a free clinic is not being considered for the new hospital, is it?" she asked.

Henry didn't say anything as he gripped the steering wheel tighter, his jaw clenched. She knew then it wasn't in the plans. The free clinic cost a lot. She was aware of that, but it was important. People died and were hurt because they couldn't afford proper care.

"It's not," he finally said. "Perhaps, if you can come up with another idea, I can persuade—"

"No. You promised me this if I pretended to be your fiancée. I'm coming to the conclusion that Aspen Grace Memorial Hospital can't be expanded. It's an old hospital."

His eyebrows raised. "So you're finally seeing that the hospital is old."

"You're right, but what I'm worried about is the people you'll alienate by opening this new hospital. People who rely on our free clinic. And that's my condition. That's why I've been protesting. I want people who can't afford to pay to be able to access health care."

"Okay."

"Okay?" she asked, shocked.

"Okay." She was pleased, but she didn't have long to relish her small victory as the car slowed down and they saw flares in the road.

"What is going on?" Henry said.

He pulled up beside a car that was on the side of the road. A man was waving his arms as they approached.

Henry rolled down the window. "Can I help?"

"Yes! Do you have a cell phone that works? I need someone to call an ambulance."

"We're doctors, what's wrong?" Henry asked, turning on his hazard lights.

"It's my wife. She's in labor and we slid off the road. The baby is coming, the car is stuck and I don't know what to do. I don't know what to do!" The man was frantic, not that Kiera could blame him.

"You call the ambulance and I'll check on the patient," she said.

"You'll what?" Henry asked, but she didn't stay to listen as she climbed out of the car. The snow was coming down heavier. Even if Henry got hold of the ambulance, it would be too late.

It would take the ambulance some time to get there and given that the man was frantic, Kiera would lay money on the fact that his wife was probably crowning.

Kiera climbed into the back seat of the car to see a woman, panting, her body covered in blankets.

"Hi, I'm Dr. Brown," she said. "Can I take a look?"

The woman nodded.

Kiera lifted the blanket and saw that the baby was indeed crowning. Yeah, the ambulance wasn't going to make it there in time.

"The ambulance is on the way. How can I help?" Henry asked.

"I need a first-aid kit, if you have it. I need some gloves or something. This baby is coming."

"I have a kit in the car." Henry disappeared.

"What's your name?" Kiera asked as she waited for Henry to come back.

"Miranda," the woman said. "Is my baby going to be okay?"

"Your baby is on the way."

"Here's the kit," Henry said. He opened it and helped her sanitize and put on gloves. She grabbed the extra blanket that was handed to her.

"Okay, Miranda when you feel that next contraction, I want you to push," Kiera said.

Miranda nodded, and Kiera could feel the contraction as she examined Miranda's belly to check on the baby.

Miranda began to push and Kiera watched, keeping her eyes on that baby.

"You're doing so well, Miranda," Kiera encouraged. "Keep going. Okay, now breathe."

The baby was coming fast, but everything looked good.

The next contraction came, and Kiera coached Miranda through it. The baby's shoulders were delivered. It took one more half push and the baby was born.

A little girl began to cry as Kiera worked. She couldn't cut the cord, because she didn't have any clamps. She could hear the ambulance siren. The paramedics could take care of that.

"It's a girl." Kiera tried to wrap the baby the best she could and handed the baby to Miranda as she waited for the placenta to be delivered, which came soon after. Once she checked it and wrapped it for the paramedics, she pulled off her gloves.

The paramedics arrived, and she watched as Henry dealt with them. She climbed out of the back of the car, slipping slightly on the snow. Henry's arms came around her to steady her.

"Good job," he whispered.

"Thanks. I'm glad we were able to help

them." Henry's arms were still around her as the paramedics finished clamping and cutting the cord and then got Miranda and her little girl out of the back of the car.

"I've called a tow truck," Henry told Miranda's husband. "I'll wait here until they come. You go with your wife and new baby."

The frantic husband smiled in appreciation. Kiera was so thankful that they had been able to help. It was a simple birth and delivery, except that it was on the side of the road, in a snowstorm, in the dark and in the back of a car. Thankfully, there had been enough blankets in the car to keep the new parents and the new baby warm on the cold winter night.

"You acted fast," Henry said. "It's been a while since I've attended a birth."

"I wouldn't think that plastic surgeons would deal with many," she replied.

"They don't. I think the last time was when I was a resident. I'm glad you were with me. I'm not sure I could have been of help."

"I didn't do anything but catch and coach the patient," Kiera said.

"I'm still glad you were there," Henry said.

"Thanks."

The ambulance drove away and they locked the car. Kiera shivered in the cold. She sat back in Henry's car and it wasn't long before he joined her. They were stuck on the side of the road waiting for a tow truck.

The only sounds were the noise of the snow blowing around and covering the windshield and the clicking sound of the car's hazard lights.

"Well, this has been an exciting night," Henry stated.

"It has. I don't think I've ever been on such a crazy date in my life," Kiera teased.

Henry laughed. "No, that was unique."

He glanced at her and her heart skipped a beat. "You did look really pretty tonight."

"Thank you." Heat flooded her cheeks.

Her pulse was thundering in her ears as they sat there next to each other in the car. She shivered.

"Here." His arm slipped around her, pulling her close. She knew she should push him away, but his arm felt nice and she stopped shivering.

And she couldn't remember the last time she'd felt something like that.

It felt good.

What was she doing?

She looked over at him. Her body was humming with anticipation. Her mouth was dry, and her breathing was fast as their gazes locked.

And before she could stop herself, she became swept up in something.

Something she didn't quite know how to control and something that she couldn't stop. And she wasn't completely sure that she wanted to stop it.

She knew it was wrong and shouldn't happen.

Kiera didn't know Henry, but in this moment she didn't want to stop the kiss from happening. His breath was hot on her neck, fanning her skin, making her aware of him. Every part of her tingled with something.

Her body was betraying her as it reacted to her enemy, to this man she didn't know and who wasn't the type of man she would ever think of going for.

This man was infuriating, privileged. He was everything she hated about this world. Yet, she didn't think he was what his parents were.

Kiera closed her eyes. She wanted him to kiss her, and her body trembled being so close to him, his strong arms around her. Her heart raced as she anticipated what it would be like to be kissed by him.

To have a kiss like this.

A forbidden kiss.

A sinful kiss. And though she should stop him, she couldn't.

His lips were gentle against hers. So many

emotions came bubbling to the surface as she sank into his kiss. Anger, guilt, lust.

Definitely lust.

That hot, heady need.

Kiera couldn't remember the last time she'd been kissed. And she certainly couldn't recall if she had ever been kissed like this before, or even if that kiss had been good, which made her think it wasn't.

Henry's kiss was all consuming.

Devouring.

She melted in his arms. She wanted him here, in the car, this man she had just met. The man who could either save everything she cared about or destroy it.

Henry's kiss made her feel like she was alive for the first time in a long time. Like she wasn't alone. Like she could have more, and that scared her.

For so long she had relied only on herself, something she'd learned at a young age. All she ever had to worry about was herself and Mandy.

And nothing else. But this kiss she was sharing with Henry made her feel safe.

What're you doing?

She pushed him away. "I can't, Henry. I'm sorry. I don't know what got into me."

"No, I'm sorry, too," he said breathlessly. "I don't know what got into me, either."

Kiera swallowed a lump in her throat, her heart still racing, her blood burning with an unquenched need.

Something she hadn't felt in such a long time.

Then they spotted flashing lights as the tow truck appeared through the heavy snow. Henry got out of the car, and the rush of cold air that blasted in calmed her down. She was able to regain some control over her emotions.

He came back to the car once the tow truck had the instructions.

"The driver said the roads are slick," Henry stated. "I'll get you home as soon as I can."

"Okay." She couldn't look at him. It was hard to look at him.

"I'm sorry for kissing you, Kiera. It won't happen again."

"Okay," she said, unsure that she didn't want that to happen again. She was relieved and disappointed at the same time, and it was a strange place to be in. "It'll be okay."

Henry nodded. "It will. I'll get you home and we can talk about this tomorrow. We can't let this affect our work."

"Sure. Sure. It won't." She straightened her shoulders. "It won't happen again."

Henry nodded and barely glanced at her as he drove back out onto the road.

It was a long, tense drive back to her place.

The snow was still falling, and as he got out to help her up the slippery ramp to her house she hoped he didn't have a long drive to wherever he was staying.

"Are you headed back up to your parents' place?" she asked.

"No. The party will still be going for a while. I have a small condo in the new part of town. It's not far from where the new hospital is supposed to be built."

She nodded. "Just be careful."

"Thanks." He smiled. "Look, we have to work together. There will be meetings, and I will do what I can for Aspen Grace Memorial Hospital, as long as you do your part."

The reminder of why they had been at the party tonight and of the deal they had worked out together brought her back to reality.

This was business.

Nothing more, and she'd been a fool to be swept up in such a trivial feeling like lust. This was a business arrangement, pure and simple.

She wasn't going to risk her heart on a chance.

She wasn't a fool.

She had walls for a reason. Walls were the things that had protected her for her whole life.

"I'll do my part. You needn't worry, Dr. Baker."

"Good night, Kiera," he said gently, and she thought she detected a hint of regret, but she pushed the thought away. She had to push him out of her mind.

There was no room for Henry.

And she had to remember that.

CHAPTER SIX

HENRY COULDN'T STOP thinking about Kiera and that kiss all night.

All he could focus on was how she had felt in his arms and how little space there was in the front of his car. How he had wanted to pull her closer to him. How he wished that they hadn't been on the side of the road waiting for a tow truck.

And how he wished that they weren't in the awkward situation of pretending to be engaged.

These were the thoughts that swirled around in his head all night.

He barely got any sleep.

He had several cold showers and went for a run on his treadmill. There was no change.

Nothing could get Kiera out of his mind.

When he'd been called to Colorado he had thought it would be an easy job. It would be no problem to shut down Dr. Brown's protest. He had foolishly thought this would be a simple thing to take care of.

Then he'd met Kiera and everything had changed in an instant.

He didn't know why he had kissed Kiera last night. It had been something he'd been fighting all night from the moment he had seen her come down the stairs in that stunning jade-colored dress. His blood heated as he thought of her in that dress.

Her long red hair tumbling down over her shoulders, the way her green eyes sparkled in the light. The pink tinge to her creamy cheeks.

The kiss flashed in his mind again.

You've got to get a hold of yourself.

He'd been doing okay all evening, resisting the urge at the party, but then he saw her climb into the back of a car and take control of a woman giving birth. She was smart and strong. Dedicated to her work, and that attracted him.

He wanted her.

Kiera was spectacular and he was overcome with an emotion, a need, that he hadn't felt in such a long time.

It scared him.

So, after tossing and turning all night, running on the treadmill and a couple of long, cold showers, he had got up as the sun was rising and had come to the hospital.

There was paperwork to do, paperwork he couldn't concentrate on. All he could think about was Kiera's lips. The taste of her. The softness of her hair as he ran his fingers through it.

Get a grip on yourself.

He dragged his hands through his hair.

He was tired of staring at the four walls of the boardroom. He needed air, and he needed to think. He usually had clarity when he was in the operating room, but he didn't have this option here.

He had no patients.

He was a surgeon with nothing to do. Normally, when he was plagued by indecision or a turmoil of emotions, he'd throw himself into his work, but that was impossible here.

So he was going a bit stir-crazy.

He needed air.

He needed to breathe.

Henry got up and opened the door of the boardroom, running smack-dab into Kiera.

"Dr. Brown!" he exclaimed. "I didn't expect to see you this morning."

"I was told you were here," she said. "And I think in public you should call me Kiera."

Henry laughed quietly. "Oh, and call you Dr. Brown in private?"

Pink tinged her cheeks, and she cocked one

of her finely arched eyebrows. "Really? We're going to do this here?"

"What can I help you with?" he asked.

"Can I come in, or are we going to continue the conversation out in the hall."

Henry stepped to the side to let Kiera enter. He shut the door behind her and turned to face her.

"So to what do I owe the pleasure this morning?" Henry asked.

She held out a folder to him. "You wanted information about the free clinic. Here it is."

Henry took the folder. "Thanks."

Henry placed the folder beside the rest of his work. She glanced at the table, her eyes widening.

"You seem to have a lot of stuff piled up."

Henry shrugged. "It's not my favorite thing, but it's something I have to do while I'm here. As a shareholder, I have a few things I need to take care of, but I loathe it. I don't mind doing charting or operative reports, but business stuff isn't as exciting."

"Then why have shares in something that makes you do what you loathe the most?"

"Because it's a hospital and I want to support medicine. I just don't like the administrative work attached to it. I'd rather be practicing medicine than balancing a budget."

What he didn't tell her was that his father actually invested the money for him. He didn't mind that his money went to a hospital, but he didn't like the work attached to it. He didn't like the hold his father had on him and he didn't know why he kept jumping.

His father was never there for him. As soon as his father was satisfied, the protests were over, and AGMH was shut down, Henry would sell all those shares his father invested for him.

He was going to sever all ties.

He was done.

Kiera cocked her head to one side. "Why don't you come down and help in the emergency room today? You said you don't get to see many general surgeries in Los Angeles, and I know that Dr. Carr would gladly give you medical privileges."

It was tempting.

He'd rather be practicing medicine than doing paperwork.

"Okay, but I don't have scrubs."

"That's an excuse," she teased. "You were able to find scrubs yesterday just fine."

"Okay then. I guess I have no excuse. Take me to where the scrubs are and get me down to the emergency room."

"Is that like take me to your leader?"

Henry rolled his eyes. "Just show me where to go."

Kiera smiled. "Follow me then."

Henry followed her out of the boardroom. He was glad for the change of pace. He was glad he'd be doing his job, the thing he was passionate about. He'd be practicing, but he was nervous that he would be working with Kiera. Especially after what had happened last night.

Especially after the kiss that was still burned on his lips.

Maybe he should go back to the boardroom.

Still, the pull of working—not thinking about his father's or his own problems—and saving lives was a delicious distraction he couldn't get enough of.

He was calm when he was saving lives and helping others.

He could clear his head when he was in the operating room.

In the operating room he didn't think about Michelle, his parents or the loneliness that consumed him.

It was like breathing for him. It was calming. It came naturally.

It was his safety.

"You know," Kiera said, breaking into his thoughts as they walked through the halls. "We're going to have to tell Dr. Carr about our engagement. I mean, if we're going public and announcing to everyone we're engaged, we should let him know. He's not only the chief of surgery, but he's like a second father to me. Next to Dr. Burke, that is."

"How do you think he'll take that?"

"Take what?" Kiera asked.

"The announcement of our engagement. I mean, I don't know him all that well, but I assume he is aware of your protests at the new hospital site."

Kiera smiled. "I do know him well and, yes, he does know about my protests. He'll be hard to sell on the idea we're engaged. I've made it clear for years that I had no interest in ever getting married."

He was intrigued by that. "No interest?"

"No. None." Only there was something about the tone of her voice that didn't quite convince him she was telling the truth. She was putting up a wall, and he understood walls. He had his own.

"Maybe I should get you a ring, and then maybe he'll believe you really are my fiancée."

Kiera paused, not sure that she'd heard him correctly.

"Pardon?" she asked, trying not to show him how shocked she actually was.

"I said maybe I should get you a ring and make it more official. More real."

Kiera opened the door to the locker room where the extra scrubs were kept. She was stunned. Her palms were suddenly very sweaty and she wished she was anywhere but here.

A ring? Was he for real?

What would she do with it? She didn't want him buying her some frivolous thing to perpetuate a lie.

That made her nervous. She didn't want to wear it.

She didn't want him to buy her anything.

"I don't want it," she said, laughing nervously as she found her voice. "I think that's the most ridiculous thing I ever heard."

A smile tugged on the corner of his lips. Lips that she had become very familiar with last night and couldn't stop thinking about this morning.

And now she was in the locker room, pulling out a pair of scrubs for him, and he was offering to buy her a ring and seemingly enjoying her discomfort over the whole thing. Which infuriated her even more.

"You think this is funny, don't you?" she asked.

"I do. I never thought you would get so worked up over a piece of jewelry. It's kind of fun."

"Fun?" She grabbed a pair of scrubs and whipped them at his face. "I'm glad you think this is fun!"

"I have to get some enjoyment out of this."

Kiera rolled her eyes but smiled. "Fine."

Henry started unbuttoning his shirt, and all she could do was stare at him. It was bad enough that she had been up half the night thinking about being in his arms and that kiss. She had a bruise on her thigh from the stick shift.

She needed to get out of there.

Only she was frozen. She couldn't move.

She turned and looked away. This had not been her plan for this morning, although she was thankful for help in the emergency room. All she had been going to do was hand Henry the report on the free clinic and then distance herself from him, because that one kiss had gotten under her skin and through her defenses.

She was obsessed by the way it had seared her soul, burned her blood.

Made her yearn for something she was afraid to reach out and take because she'd been burned before.

Usually she could resist, but for some reason she couldn't resist Henry.

It rattled her.

And she didn't like to be rattled.

All she wanted to do was bury herself in

work. If she kept busy in the emergency room and the operating room, she wouldn't have to see him until she collected herself. Until she stopped thinking about the kiss that had fired her blood and sizzled through her system all night long.

Work would help cleanse that. It would help her focus.

She could get clarity from saving lives.

It didn't matter that Dr. Henry Baker working with her in the operating room and offering her a ring had not been on the agenda.

The whole idea was silly.

"You can look now, I'm changed," he teased. "Though, if you are my fiancée, you really shouldn't be embarrassed if I'm changing in front of you."

She glared at him. "You know what? I really like the grumpy, nonverbal, moody side of you, Dr. Baker."

He laughed. "And I kind of like getting under your skin a bit, Dr. Brown."

Kiera rolled her eyes. "Just follow me and try to stay out of my way today."

"I'll try, but you know if we're going to convince my parents that we're engaged, we're going to have to seem a bit friendlier toward one another."

"Don't I know it," she grumbled. She pushed

the button to open the automatic double doors that led into the emergency room. Triage was busy, but it was mostly just people with minor ailments, and as soon as she saw that she frowned. "I wonder why they're not at the free clinic?"

"The free clinic was shut down," a nurse said, hearing her and passing by.

"What?" Kiera asked, shocked, spinning around to Henry.

He put up his hands. "I didn't shut it down."

"Then who did?" Kiera asked. "What's going on?"

"I shut it down," Dr. Carr said, coming over to them. "By an order from the chairman of the board."

Henry looked confused. "I am chairman of the board."

Richard nodded. "And yesterday you told me to shut it down."

"I didn't, though."

Kiera was having a hard time believing him, and she didn't want to stand around discussing this. It was making her too angry.

"I have patients to see," she muttered, and walked away.

She couldn't look at him right now. She didn't want to look at him. She felt betrayed.

He had probably ordered it to shut down before they'd made their deal, but it still stung.

Henry followed after her.

"Kiera, I didn't order it to be shut down."

"I'm sure."

He frowned. "You don't believe me."

"Any reason why I *should* believe you? I don't know you."

He grabbed her arm. "You do. Remember?"

Kiera sighed. "You know what I meant."

Henry leaned forward. "I know that, but others don't—be careful."

She wanted to discuss it further, but the ambulance bay door opened and the paramedics wheeled in a patient.

"Twenty-three-year-old man. Third-degree burns over his face and his right arm."

Henry left and was instantly at the patient's side. Kiera followed as they wheeled the unconscious patient into a trauma room for workup.

"GCS in the field was a five. The patient has smoke inhalation. He was in a house fire," the paramedic said.

Kiera examined the man's nose and throat and saw evidence that smoke had infiltrated the lungs. "I need to intubate him."

Kiera grabbed a laryngoscope and visualized the cords as she grabbed the endotracheal tube and placed it down his throat.

A nurse used an Ambu bag to keep the patient breathing as Kiera listened with a stethoscope for breath sounds. She smiled, listening to the equal breath sounds. The patient was successfully intubated.

"These burns are bad. I'll wrap them and we'll treat the patient once he gets to the intensive care unit," Henry said.

Kiera nodded. She took some blood and sent it off to be tested for carbon monoxide.

She didn't say anything else to Henry. There was nothing much more to say though she couldn't get over the sick feeling in the pit of her stomach. Henry was quiet as he carefully cared for the patient's burns.

Once they were wrapped, they took the patient to the intensive care unit, got him registered and talked with the victim's family.

Now it would be a waiting game. The patient had high levels of carbon monoxide in his blood.

The hairs on his face and his nose were singed and when she was intubating him Kiera could see the smoke inhalation damage. He'd be in the intensive care unit until his lungs could heal.

"I'll change the dressings tomorrow," Henry said as he finished giving instructions to the intensive care nurses.

Aspen Grace Memorial Hospital didn't have

a large intensive care unit, but they had a good one. Of course, they had a great free clinic, too.

"Do you think you forgot you ordered it closed?" Kiera asked.

"What?" Henry asked.

"The free clinic."

"I didn't have it shut down, Kiera. I didn't have time after I arrived."

"But Richard said the chairman of the board shut it down. You are chairman of the board."

"But I didn't do it," Henry snapped.

"Henry didn't, I did."

Kiera spun around and saw Governor Baker standing there.

Henry's spine stiffened. "Father."

CHAPTER SEVEN

"Do you mind telling me what's going on, Henry?" his father demanded as soon as they were behind closed doors. Kiera had returned to the emergency room because his father didn't want her to be part of the discussion.

"Do you mind telling me why I've been removed as chair?" Henry barked back.

"You're engaged to Dr. Brown—the person I sent you to stop from protesting. You're a liability to the project now."

"Hardly. Kiera has some good insights regarding the hospital. Insights that you and I don't have."

"You're a doctor. Are you telling me you don't have insight?"

"Not at this hospital. I suppose I've been rendered useless to you again."

His father rolled his eyes. "Please... She's using you. Can't you see that, Henry?"

Henry tried not to react to the kernel of truth

his father was spouting. He'd been used before and he was not unfamiliar with it.

Yes, Kiera was agreeing to be his fiancée while he was in town, but he was using her, too.

Using her as a shield to annoy his father. Clearly, it was working.

He knew what was happening here.

The problem was that she was slipping past his walls, and he was afraid of being hurt.

He was also afraid of hurting her when this was over.

She's not into you. You won't hurt her.

Kiera was strong. She didn't need him, even if he needed her, and the thought spooked him because he had enjoyed being with her last night.

That kiss was something he wouldn't soon forget.

He liked being around her, and he resented his father for forcing him to put a stop on things.

"She's not right for you," his father said.

"I say she is."

And it gave him satisfaction he had chosen Kiera in the heat of the moment.

The woman his father apparently loathed.

Of course, his father hadn't liked Michelle much, either, because Michelle had been a strong woman, and that had driven his father crazy. His father detested strong women.

His father didn't want anyone defying him.

Which was all the more reason Henry was glad that it annoyed his father so much that he was engaged to Kiera.

And why he liked Kiera even more.

You're not really engaged to her, though.

And he had to remind himself of that.

Kiera wouldn't like him if she knew why he was here. That he had been sent to deal with her because of his past and the deal he had made with his father. She wouldn't like him if she knew that he planned to walk away from Aspen Grace Memorial Hospital and Colorado for good once this was over.

"What're you doing here, Father?" Henry asked. "You pulled me from my work in Los Angeles, and now you swoop in to do my job for me?"

"I came here because I saw you were with Dr. Brown at our fundraiser and couldn't quite believe it when your mother told me you were engaged to her. To our enemy. The one thorn in our side, standing in the way of our new hospital."

"She's your enemy, not mine."

His father's eyes narrowed. "I thought you wanted me to forget about your indiscretions?"

"I do."

"This is not what I had in mind. You owe me, Henry."

"I'm working on it," Henry gritted out.

"How? You're engaged to the woman I asked you to stop! Did she blackmail you or something?"

"No. She's not like you."

His father grinned, but it wasn't a warm, happy grin. It was cold, calculating, the kind Henry was used to.

"Be careful, Henry. You have a task to do. Complete it."

"I will."

"I'm not convinced. Need I remind you that you're a majority shareholder in this hospital. Her blocking the new building threatens your investment, too." Which was true, but Henry didn't care as much as he had before.

"Kiera is prepared to discuss the new hospital if the free clinic stays open."

That had his father's attention. "The free clinic?"

Henry nodded. "Since I'm no longer the chairman, you'll find all the paperwork in the boardroom. Including a report on the free clinic. Now, if you don't mind, I have patients to attend to."

His father stepped in front of him. "Fine. I'll look at the report, but you and Kiera need to be seen."

"What're you talking about?" Henry asked, confused.

"It would help the board's reputation if you were seen out and about with Kiera. It would show our support for Aspen."

"I thought it angered you when I was in the papers in Los Angeles," he smirked.

"This is different."

"How?"

"She's a respected doctor in Aspen."

"You mean it would look good for your political career," Henry stated.

His father shrugged. "It couldn't hurt."

"No. That's not part of the deal."

"It is now since you bungled the original task. Get your picture taken with her. Announce your engagement. It'll look good, and then maybe we can consider the free clinic in the new hospital. Maybe."

Henry seethed.

All that mattered to his father was his political career.

Why was he shocked about this?

He wasn't. He was angry that Kiera was involved because of him, because he had thought it would annoy his father the most. Now Kiera had been sucked into his father's agenda even more.

Kiera didn't deserve this, and neither did he.

"We're done talking about this."

"Henry, I invested those shares for you. Don't make me regret my generosity."

The threat sent a chill down his spine.

If he lost the shares, then he couldn't help Kiera and she wouldn't want to be around him. The only reason they were together was because he'd promised to help her. Their engagement was fake.

And if he couldn't, why would she stay with him?

What do you expect?

It shouldn't bother him, but it did.

He was angry.

Henry didn't respond and left the room. Frustrated.

He headed back to the emergency room, and though he should put some distance between Kiera and his uncontrolled emotions, he sought her out.

He hated losing control. Control kept the grief, the hurt, the loneliness at bay. Kiera was a balm to soothe his soul.

A balm that had a bit of a bite to it, but once you got past that burn, it was so good.

She finished up with a patient and walked over to the desk to input information. He crept up beside her, and she glanced up at him and raised her eyebrows.

"Whoa, that is some serious, dark, twisty energy coming off you."

"Want to go out?" he asked.

"What?" she asked, chuckling.

"Tonight. My place. Nothing fancy and I'll cook."

Her mouth dropped open and pink bloomed in her cheeks. "Okay…yeah. That sounds good."

"Good. I'll see you at seven. I'll text you the address."

And then he left the emergency room. He had to gain some clarity, some control of the emotions raging inside him.

And he had to make dinner, though he had no idea what.

He wasn't the best cook, and the last thing he needed was the papers proclaiming he'd poisoned his fiancée in some kind of scheme. He laughed at the paranoid thought.

You can do this.

And he could.

More importantly, he wanted to.

Kiera drove up to Henry's condo. He'd said it wasn't far from the main part of town, but it wasn't as close as she thought. She still had steep roads to negotiate and it was snowing, heavily, again.

His condo was in a newer part of town, a

new alpine village. Another place for skiers to come and ski.

Another resort that catered to the elite.

The shops that lined the quaint little street were exclusive and unaffordable. Kiera parked her car in the village parking lot and walked up through the village that sat at the base of a ski lift. Henry's condo overlooked the mountain where all the happier skiers were enjoying a perfectly snowy night.

After she typed in his code and the entry door opened, she made her way to the elevator. The elevator took her to the sixth floor, which was the penthouse of this strange modern condo that looked so out of place in Aspen.

The elevator opened, and she was shocked as she walked straight into an open concept apartment that resembled a rustic ski chalet—with exposed wood beams, the floor-to-ceiling windows and a crackling fire put in the middle of a sunken living room.

Henry came out of the kitchen and her heart skipped a beat. She had thought he looked good in a power suit and tuxedo, but those outfits had nothing on seeing him in a pair of well-fitted jeans and a blue sweater.

The sweater was such a beautiful blue and brought out the color of his eyes. Made his brown eyes, deeper. Like mahogany. His hair was tousled and there were a few stray curls.

"You found it okay then." He took her coat.

"This place looks completely differently from the outside," she said, still stunned.

"It's why I like it."

"So this is your home away from Los Angeles?"

He nodded. "It is. I bought it a while ago, but rarely come here."

"You didn't want to stay at your parents'?"

"No," he said tightly, hanging up her coat.

"Well, I do like this place. It's open, but also warm and cozy."

Kiera followed him into the penthouse and down the steps of the sunken living room that was giving off a retro chalet vibe.

The fire felt good as she perched on the edge of his large sectional couch.

"Can I get you a glass of wine?" he asked.

"Yes. Thank you."

Henry headed into the kitchen area and Kiera relaxed.

"So, I'm intrigued about why you were so adamant in wanting to cook for me tonight," she said, trying to make conversation.

"Well, my father is convinced you're using me. And if we're going to continue with this ruse, I thought it best we got to know one another." He came back and handed her a glass of red wine.

"Is the wine to numb the pain?" she teased.

He smiled, a twinkle in his eyes. "Perhaps."

"Well, it's a good start."

She didn't like people, other than Mandy and Dr. Carr, to know too much about her. It was too painful. When she had let down her guard in the past, in particular as she had with Brent, she'd been hurt. People couldn't be trusted. They always left in the end, always disappointed you.

They were selfish for the most part.

Even she was selfish. She was only helping Henry out to get something from him.

And she didn't trust Henry; however, she was beginning to relax with him, and it was scary. She couldn't let him in. She just couldn't get hurt again.

"I'll go first. I'm forty," he said, breaking through her morose thoughts.

Kiera laughed. "I did know that tidbit."

"How?"

"I did research on you before you came to Aspen, and I'm sure your father's people have quite the dossier on me."

Henry chuckled. "Most likely, but I'm not privy to it. So you probably know more about me than I do about you."

"Okay, well what do you want to know?"

Kiera hoped her voice didn't shake as she said that, because she really didn't like sharing personal information with anyone.

She hadn't had much privacy growing up and she liked to keep things close to her chest.

She didn't like to even remember her parents or her past. She didn't like reliving it. Those had been dark times. Wilfred and Mandy had made her life happy.

There was no need to think about the father who had abandoned her.

The person she had waited to come back for so long, and he never had.

She'd moved on.

Have you?

"Well, you said Dr. Burke raised you but isn't your father. Are you related to him?" Henry asked.

Kiera tried to swallow the wine caught in her throat.

"Wow, you really get to the heart of the matter."

"We're engaged, so I guess I should know about where you came from."

Kiera sighed. Her hands were shaking, her pulse was racing, and she felt sick.

"No, I'm not related to Wilfred Burke or Mandy."

"You seem nervous."

"I am." She set down the wineglass. "I don't… I don't think about it."

She trailed off as she thought about her past. Her mother had been so addicted to drugs that she'd died in an emergency room from an overdose, and her father had been unable to cope, either. He had left her in a dingy diner in Colorado Springs.

Kiera had sat there for hours, waiting for her dad to come back.

And he never had.

She'd probably be dead if she had stayed with her biological father. She would have started using. No one would have helped her, and she certainly wouldn't have become a doctor.

It had been the scariest moment of her life, but eventually she'd come to Aspen, and Dr. Burke and Mandy had taken her in.

"I'm not an orphan," she said quickly clearing her throat. "My mother died, but my father abandoned me at a roadside diner."

Henry's expression softened. "I'm sorry."

"Don't pity me," she said quickly. She hated the pity. There was no need for it. Not once Wilfred and Mandy became her family.

She was lucky really.

"This is me doing anything but."

Her heart skipped a beat. A flush of warmth spread through her. Usually people pitied her if they found out about her past, but she could tell that Henry didn't because he looked her in the eye and reached out to take her hand. It caused her to gasp slightly, shocked that he was reaching out to touch her instead of being uncomfortable with her past. She didn't pull away from the touch.

It made her feel safe.

Men she'd dated in the past had felt sorry for her once they knew about her past. She was not defined by her past. Only her present, but no one could see beyond her biological parents' tainted past.

It was another reason she didn't share anything about herself. She didn't trust anyone with her pain.

And she didn't want to let people in.

It was easier to stay single. To be alone.

Yet, here she was, engaged.

Not really engaged.

And she had to keep reminding herself of that. They were exchanging information in order to keep up the subterfuge.

"So that's my past. I was an abandoned kid who grew up in the system until a kindly widowed man with a daughter the same age as me took me in."

"How did Dr. Burke find you?" Henry asked.

"He became a foster parent. I was struggling

in other homes and he chose me." She smiled as she thought of Wilfred. "I'll be eternally grateful. I was alone for so long."

"I can relate to that," Henry said, sliding close to her.

"I know that you can't. You had two parents."

"Two absent parents. I grew up in boarding schools and servants raised me."

"Similar, but not the same." Kiera took another sip of her wine.

"How do you mean?" he asked.

"You were still cared for."

"But not by my parents. They might not have physically abandoned me, but emotionally they did."

She melted because he understood her. He knew what it was like and tears welled up in her eyes. They were unwelcome. She didn't cry in front of anyone.

The only time she'd cried was when Wilfred died and she'd been with him after he passed.

He had told no one he was so sick, and Kiera hadn't made it in time to say goodbye, to thank him.

He had lain there. Calm. Peaceful. The nurses had told her what was wrong with him. They had told her about the cancer that had ravaged him. She had been allowed to be alone in the room with him. No longer was he in pain, and all she could do was drop to her knees and weep.

"I'm sorry," she whispered, her voice trembling as she tried to banish the memory from her mind so she didn't cry in front of him. "I guess we are the same in some ways."

"Well, this is kind of a bummer. How about something to eat? I made…something I'm not that sure of."

Kiera laughed, the sadness ebbing away. "Something that you're not sure of? That sounds appetizing."

"I wouldn't bet on it."

Kiera followed Henry into his kitchen. His kitchen was clean and looked like it had barely been used. It looked brand-new.

The kitchen at her place was used. Well used. Kiera could cook a few things, but Mandy did most of the cooking.

This kitchen looked like it just plopped itself out of a factory.

"Why do I smell plastic?" Kiera asked.

"What?" Henry opened the oven and she could see a rotisserie chicken from a grocery store, still sitting in its plastic container. The plastic container was melting and dribbling down into some kind bubbly orange and green side dish.

She stifled a laugh. "You know that those

chickens from the grocery store are actually cooked, right?"

"Yeah, well, it needed to be warmed." Henry grabbed his oven mitts, still with the price tag on them, and pulled out the melted plastic holding the destroyed chicken. And then pulled out another dish, a discolored, hardened casserole of some sort.

"What was that supposed to be?" she asked as she came to stand beside him and inspect the trauma more carefully. She was a trauma doctor, after all, and assessing the damage was part of her job.

And there was a lot of carnage here in this mystery side dish.

"It was supposed to be a sweet potato casserole."

"What's with the green?" she asked, wrinkling her nose and leaning over him.

"Spinach. I added spinach, I thought they might go well together. Apparently, I was wrong."

"You were so wrong. So, so very wrong."

"Well, I guess there goes my idea of cooking you dinner. The whole reason for inviting you here was to do that. Michelle always told me I was a terrible cook…" He trailed off and something changed.

He was no longer laughing. He walked away from the chicken and the sweet potato casserole.

"Who's Michelle?" she asked gently.

"I don't want to talk about it," he said quietly. "I didn't mean to mention her."

"Look, I told you about my past, tell me about Michelle, because obviously she is someone important. Someone a fiancée would know about?"

Henry ran his hands through his hair. "I don't talk about her, and I didn't…"

"I don't talk about my past," she said softly. "You didn't pity me, and I promise not to pity you."

She could tell it was difficult for him. It was something that stung him deeply.

Henry looked back at her. His eyes were dark, and all the mirth, relaxation and happiness that had been there a moment ago when they had been laughing over the chicken was gone.

It was replaced with pain.

"Michelle was my fiancée. She died."

"I'm sorry for your loss. How did she die? May I ask that?"

"She was a surgeon, as well. A trauma surgeon who worked with a search and rescue team. She really liked going into remote locations and saving lives. One day, she went in to help and there was an accident. She was in a remote spot and the small clinic there couldn't handle her injuries. So she succumbed to them. Even if she made it, I doubt she could've survived, now looking back. She might've had a chance, but who knows."

It was then that it hit her why he was in favor of building a bigger hospital, a better hospital. A larger emergency room, a bigger intensive care unit and a teaching program. When he looked at Aspen Grace Memorial Hospital he saw the sort of small hospital that couldn't save the woman he loved.

Her heart melted for him a bit.

It wasn't about money. It wasn't about making more money.

For Henry, it was something deep and personal.

And she understood that.

She wanted to save the free clinic because of what had happened to Mandy; Henry wanted to make sure that Aspen Grace Memorial Hospital was the best it could be.

"I'm sorry."

"Don't be." He scrubbed his hand over his face. "Well, now we know our deep, dark secrets. What do we do with this?"

Kiera sighed. "I don't know. We certainly can't eat dinner, because it's kind of horrific."

A smile quirked the corner of his lips. "Well, that's for sure."

"I still can't believe you tried to cook a cooked chicken."

"Shut up." The twinkle returned to his eyes. "Do you like pizza?"

"I could go for some pizza."

"There's a good place near the base of the mountain, by the main lodge. Would you like to take a walk there?"

"I would like that." And she would. She was enjoying her time with him.

"Let's go then."

Kiera followed Henry. He helped her with her coat, pulled on his jacket, and they took the elevator in silence down to street level.

It was snowing pretty heavily, but that wasn't stopping people from walking through the shops that lined the street. Although Kiera loathed these new mountain resorts and vacation timeshares that were built to cater to the elite, she did like the fact that they resembled perfect Christmas villages.

Except that it was February.

Still, it was nice to walk through the village. It was snowing heavily and there was no wind. Just big, fat, fluffy snowflakes.

"I hate the snow," Henry grumbled.

"Why?"

"It's cold."

"You said you were born in Colorado. I mean your dad is governor currently and Colorado is his home state. I'd have thought you would be used to the cold."

"I've lived in Los Angeles for eight years. I've rarely come to Colorado since then, so I don't think I'm acclimatized to it. That, and I really never did like the cold." The cold reminded him of being alone. "Sure we had servants, but I was alone in a dreary house on top of a mountain. The wind scared me. So I've never been a fan of winter."

"I wasn't born here, but I don't mind the cold."

"Where were you born?" he asked.

"Helena," she teased. "So, nowhere with a warmer climate."

Henry opened the door to the pizza shop and a blast of warm air hit her in the face. The smell of actual, properly cooked food wafted toward her, making her stomach growl.

"We'll take care of that," he teased, obviously hearing her tummy rumble.

And her cheeks flushed, realizing he'd heard that.

"How about since you tried so hard and bought the wine, I buy dinner?"

"Deal."

Henry didn't like talking about Michelle, and he didn't know why he had opened up about it.

That was something he kept close to his heart. It was his pain to bear and he didn't want to share it with anyone else. It was something that he lived with, it reminded him to keep his heart in check.

That he couldn't put himself on the line like that.

He didn't know what it was about Kiera that brought it all out again. Maybe it was knowing her past, too, that made it easier. Kiera had got under his skin, from the moment she had climbed into the back of his father's car with that ridiculous protest sign.

When he thought of that sign, with his father's picture painted with devil horns, he chuckled.

He really didn't know what it was about Kiera, but he knew he liked being with her. She made him forget about a lot of things—he felt alive.

And he wasn't so alone. He laughed more. It had been a while since he had really laughed.

He hadn't realized how lonely he actually was.

Kiera slid into the booth across from him. "Pizza will be here soon."

"Good."

"It doesn't have plastic in it," she teased.

"That's always good."

"So, you must have a cook in Los Angeles."

"No, I just go out a lot or order in, that's if I'm at home. I spend a lot of time at my clinic. I work a lot."

"So do I."

"How does Mandy feel about that?" he asked.

"She gets lonely, but I love my work and… I learned from Dr. Burke, and he was always there for his patients. Working reminds me of him and I don't miss him as much. Besides, Mandy always encourages me to go out."

That struck a chord with him. He understood that.

Henry nodded. "So what kind of pizza did you order for us?"

"Well, for me I ordered just pepperoni, but for you, I added spinach."

Henry laughed with her.

It was good to laugh with her.

It was good not to be alone.

They finished the pizza and made their way back. Henry offered to walk her to her car. The snow was coming down harder. When they got closer to the parking lot, there were flashing lights.

"What's going on?" Kiera asked.

"I don't know."

It was the state troopers, and there was a roadblock up.

"Officer, is there a problem?" Henry asked.

"The road is shut down. There was an avalanche."

"We're doctors—was anyone injured?" Kiera asked.

"No, ma'am. The road is blocked, though, and we're asking everyone to stay put for now. It probably won't be clear until the morning. Do you have a place to stay? If not, the mountain lodge is setting up cots and a warming station."

"She has a place to stay. Thank you, Officer," Henry said.

He put his arm around Kiera and led her away from the parking lot.

"I guess I should find a place in the mountain lodge," she said.

"Why, when I have a perfectly good place?" he asked.

"Do you think that's wise?"

"Kiera, we're engaged. I think it's safe."

Kiera worried her bottom lip. "Okay. I guess you have a point."

"Come on. It'll be fine. We'll watch a movie and hunker down until the road is clear."

Kiera nodded, and they walked back to his place.

His pulse was racing. He only had one bed. He'd give that to Kiera and sleep on the couch, but for tonight, he was glad that Kiera was staying over.

He'd enjoyed his time with her.

And he was glad that, tonight, he wouldn't be alone.

CHAPTER EIGHT

"I SEE A huge problem here," Kiera said.

"The one bed thing?" Henry asked.

"Yes." She had her arms crossed and she was staring at the bed like it was on fire. Tonight had been lovely, and getting to know her better had made him want her more, but he had to resist. This wasn't real.

His attraction might be, but their relationship wasn't.

Sharing a bed was out of the question.

"I don't expect to share a bed," he said quickly. "I want you to have the bed."

"Are you sure?"

"Yes. Of course, I may be the villain who swooped in, is threatening to shut down your hospital and has persuaded you to pose as my fiancée, but I am a gentleman first and foremost."

"And where will you sleep?"

"On the couch."

Kiera frowned. "That couch doesn't look comfortable at all."

"It's fine." He reached into a drawer and handed her one of his T-shirts and a pair of jogging pants. The jogging pants were probably going to be too big for her, but at least she wouldn't have to wear her jeans to bed and be uncomfortable.

And she wouldn't be sleeping naked or in her underwear, and he wouldn't have to think about that. Like he was thinking about it now.

Get a hold of yourself.

It was bad enough that he was thinking about her sleeping in his bed.

That she was spending the night.

So close.

He had to get a grip.

"You sleep here and I'll sleep out on the couch, and hopefully tomorrow morning the roads will be cleared and you can head back home."

"Okay. Thanks." She sounded nervous as she held his spare pair of jogging pants tight to her chest.

Henry nodded. "And I promise you that I won't try to cook you breakfast in the morning."

Kiera laughed, breaking the tension. "Okay, deal."

"Good night." He grabbed a pillow and a blanket from his closet, leaving Kiera alone in his bedroom. He shut the door.

He sighed and made his way to the couch. His condo was dark, and the only light filtering through was the light from the mountain through the heavy snow and the dwindling fire, since he'd turned the gas down low.

He stretched himself out on the couch and tried to get comfortable, but it was hard. His couch might be a sectional, but a sectional wasn't long enough in one direction for him to get comfortable, and he really didn't want to fold himself in half to get a good night's sleep.

Even if the couch were twenty feet long and twenty feet wide he was pretty sure that he wouldn't sleep well. Not when Kiera was so close. Her hand on his pillow. Her scent on his sheets. He couldn't stop thinking about how nice it was to have her here.

To talk to someone.

He rolled over to try and get comfortable.

But when he closed his eyes, all he could think about was her in that jade dress and the kiss they'd shared in his car.

Just like he had done the night before. He had spent a restless night then and would now. It was the last sleepless night that had led to this moment, the result of making a rash decision and inviting her over for dinner. Now Kiera was sleeping in his bed, and he was here on the couch, and all he could think about was her.

You didn't plan the avalanche.

It didn't matter. She was here, invading his space.

Henry tried to turn on his side and couldn't. The couch was too narrow.

There was a creak behind him and he sat up.

"Kiera?" he asked.

She was standing in the dark, in his sweats and an oversize shirt, her hair braided over her shoulder. She looked even better than she had all dressed up.

"Yeah, I couldn't sleep, and I felt bad that I had your bed. I was going to see if you had any milk. Warm milk usually helps me fall asleep."

"I do have milk." He pulled back the blanket and got up.

"You don't have to get up. I can make warmed milk—in fact, I'd rather make it."

"I can't sleep. So why don't you make me a cup, too."

Kiera nodded and made her way into the kitchen. Henry sat down at the counter as Kiera pulled out a saucepan. She poured milk into the saucepan and started rooting through his bare cupboards.

"What're you looking for?" he asked. "The mugs are hanging up in front of you."

"I'm looking for cinnamon." She frowned. "You don't have any."

"I don't cook. Remember? The remnants of that casserole you called traumatic is in my trash can."

Kiera chuckled and pulled out a spoon to stir the milk. "Right. I forgot that you eat out."

"I was never taught the basic skills of cooking. Boarding school, servants and privilege, remember?"

"I remember. Well, why don't you come over here and I'll teach you how to stir some warm milk."

Henry got up and came up behind her. He could smell the lavender in her hair and it fired his senses though he resisted the urge to reach out and touch her as he stared down at the graceful curve of her neck.

"If you don't stir it often, it will burn."

"What?" he asked, shaking his head.

"The milk." She glanced up at him and there was a pink tinge to her cheeks. He was standing so close to her and all he could think about was kissing her.

He didn't really care about the milk or the hospital or the fact that his father was threatening to take away his shares. Shares he planned to sell anyway, and he'd give every red cent back to his father.

He didn't care that he had shared too much of himself today.

He didn't care about any of that.

All he could think about was the fact that Kiera was here. So close to him, wearing his clothes, and he could smell her hair.

"Stir the milk." He cleared his throat and took a step back "Right. Got it."

"If you had cinnamon, it would taste a heck of a lot better," she said, turning off the stove and pulling down a mug so she could pour a cup for him.

He really didn't give a hoot about the milk right now. It was a distraction from the fact that he wanted to kiss her.

Henry took his mug and wandered away from the kitchen, back to the couch. He sat down with his drink, which really tasted like sawdust in his mouth.

Kiera came over and sat down on the far side of the couch, cupping her mug as she sipped at it.

"It really would be better with cinnamon," she said.

"I've never had warm milk before."

"We're going to have a conversation about warm milk?" she teased.

"No. I really don't want that. What I'd like is sleep."

"This couch looks great in here, but it's not exactly comfortable, is it?"

"I know. I'm getting old and I'm not used to sleeping on a couch anymore."

Kiera smiled at him. "Why don't you come and sleep in your bed?"

His pulse skipped a beat, and he wasn't sure he had heard her correctly. "What?"

"We'll share. We're adults. We can share a king-size bed, and you have enough pillows for a sufficient pillow wall."

Kiera couldn't believe she'd just invited Henry into bed. To share a bed with her because she couldn't get to sleep, even though she was incredibly tired. Henry had shared so much about himself.

He was just like her.

And she did feel so alone. She could feel her barriers slipping.

It was scary, but she was lonely on the other side of the high walls she'd built for herself.

She had been hoping he'd still be awake, and even though she should have just stayed in his room and tried to sleep, she couldn't. So she'd gotten up.

And as she was making the warm milk she

was very aware of Henry standing close to her. She had also been very aware that she was sleeping in his bed.

Even though he had changed the sheets, she could smell him.

She could sense him. Everywhere.

All she'd been able to do was toss and turn, just like the previous night. Now she was wearing his clothes.

And more... She was sharing a drink with him and inviting him back to bed.

With her.

What had come over her?

What was wrong with her?

Ever since Henry had landed in Aspen and pulled her off her protest site, she'd been distracted.

She shouldn't have come here tonight.

She should've just stayed home.

Only she hadn't. She was here now, and she'd opened up to him and felt vulnerable and exposed. And now she was inviting him to share a bed.

She didn't know what she was thinking, but right now they were both tired, and there was a large bed they both could sleep on together.

"Let's go to bed." She set down her mug. "I'm pretty good at building pillow walls."

"Okay." He set down his mug and grabbed his blankets and his pillow.

Her heart was hammering in her chest like a jackhammer. It thundered between her ears, and she wondered if he could hear it, too.

She was nervous.

She'd dated men before, she'd slept with men before, but somehow this was different, and she couldn't figure out why.

It's just sharing a bed. That's all.

Kiera headed over to his bed to grab a few pillows, keeping one for her head as she set up a wall.

"You *are* good at pillow walls," Henry said as she walked around the bed and sat down on the opposite side of the wall.

"See, this can be done." Kiera pulled the blanket up. "We're adults. We can be civilized, and we can both get a good night's sleep."

Henry didn't respond, and when she peered over the pillow wall, she saw that he was lying on his back, his eyes closed, sleeping.

She smiled, watching him sleep in the darkness, just the light from outside casting shadows across his face. He looked kind of peaceful, this man who could be threatening her hospital, and her free clinic.

When she had heard that he was coming to Aspen, she had hated him. Hated the thought of him, but now that she had got to know him, it was different.

She understood him.

And that scared her. What if he abandoned her like her father had? Like Brent had?

What if Henry found someone else? Back in California it appeared he had multiple women and never for very long.

Brent had left her—what was stopping Henry from doing the same?

They were very similar, yet different. Her heart would break if Henry broke her trust. Of that she was certain.

This isn't real. You have nothing to be afraid of.

The problem was it felt real, and she secretly wanted it to be.

She relaxed against the pillow and tried not to think about the fact that he was so close to her, that he was within an arm's reach of her and that she was in his bed.

Kiera's eyes closed.

And she tried to sleep.

Kiera was vaguely aware of an arm around her and something curled up behind her. Something warm, and she didn't want to get out of bed. It was nice.

And then the realization hit her that she

wasn't in her bed, because the thing that was curled up against her wasn't Sif the cat.

She opened one eye, saw Henry's arm wrapped around her and realized that he was spooning her. She slowly peered over her shoulder and saw that he was still sleeping and that the pillow wall was gone and spread out all over the floor. It felt so good to be wrapped up in his arms and she couldn't believe how soundly she had slept, but she had to get out of there.

Preferably before Henry woke up and it was all awkward.

She wanted to move, but she also didn't want to wake him up. She had to think of an easy way to slip out from under his arm without waking him, and she wasn't quite sure how she was going to do that.

Kiera started shimmying down under the blanket, trying to scoot under the crutch of his arm and the blankets to the end of the bed, where her plan was then to drop to the floor. As she slowly crept under the covers toward freedom at the end of the bed, she was thankful for the few Pilates classes she had taken.

What she hadn't counted on was the blankets and sheets still being tightly tucked in at the foot of the bed. And she hadn't thought there was a footboard on the bed frame, but there was and she was trapped, curled up in a ball at the end of the bed like some kind of freak.

"Um, Kiera?"

"Yeah?" she answered nervously.

Henry peeked under the blanket. "What're you doing?"

"Trying not to wake you up?" she offered.

He chuckled. "Mission accomplished."

"Ha-ha."

He disappeared and rolled away, and she clambered out from under the blankets that were now tangled around her legs.

He'd retreated to his side of the bed.

"So much for your pillow wall."

"Hey, my pillow walls are usually fantastic."

He smirked. "I have to say this was a first for me."

"What, pillow walls?"

"Usually I'm the one sneaking out of the bed in the mornings."

Heat flushed her cheeks at being caught, but there was a pang of jealousy there, too. The thought of him with someone else. Or multiple someones. And she was surprised over the little green-eyed monster that sprang up.

Why should she care?

This wasn't a real relationship.

She knew this about him. She knew the kind of women he usually dated.

"Good for you," she replied sarcastically. What she didn't tell him was that in the past she had been the one to sneak out of the bed when she slept with a man. The only differences were there hadn't been many men and it hadn't happened for a long time.

She didn't like sleeping over with her dates, but leaving in the morning gave her a chance to leave before they left her.

And with the way she had opened up to Henry, she was in full-on panic mode. She wanted to put some distance between him and herself.

She needed to get back to the hospital.

She had to remember why she was dating Henry, or rather why she was fake dating Henry. It was for the free clinic and those patients who needed her. And last night he'd made her forget all those things.

For one fraction of a second she had thought she was on a real date. She had forgotten what this was all about. It wasn't real.

And the only reason they had opened up and shared was to keep up the lie.

He was making her lose control, because she didn't share this stuff with anyone. Not even Mandy.

And that unnerved her. Since she needed

to calm herself down and practicing medicine helped her, she needed to get out of there. She needed space.

"Where are you sneaking off to anyways?" he asked.

"I've got patients to check up on and some rounds," she said quickly. "So if the road is open I should get back to the hospital."

"Okay." He was lying there on his back, bare chested, so that she could see his finely sculpted chest and abs, his arm behind his head, looking devilishly sexy. The tattoo on his forearm was indeed a tree, but she tried not to stare at it or him, because if she focused too long on him, her stomach would start flipping with anticipation.

She stared at the sheets, instead, the nice Egyptian cotton sheets, until she realized the bed was rumpled as if they had spent the night making love.

A zing of heat coursed through her.

When was the last time she had that kind of release?

It had been too long.

They hadn't, but the very thought of it made her body react. A rush of blood to her groin, her palms sweaty.

Great. Just great.

Yeah, she had to get out of there—and fast.

Kiera grabbed her clothes. "Thanks for dinner."

"You mean thanks for not actually poisoning you?" he teased, sitting up.

"Yeah. That. I'll get dressed and see myself out. Will I see you at the hospital later?"

Henry nodded. "Yes."

"Okay. Thanks again." She retreated from the bedroom to the guest bathroom down the hall.

She was quick about getting changed, cleaned up, and once she found her coat and purse she slipped out of the building and into the cold. Outside the snow was deep, but the plow had been by. All she had to do was scrape off her car and head back into town.

She'd get back to work and forget all about how good it had actually felt to wake up in Henry's arms. And how scared that made her feel.

She was lonely. She knew that, but she could deal with it. She knew how to be alone. She'd been alone most of her life.

She had learned to not rely on anyone.

Except Mandy, but even then, it was Mandy who relied on her.

Does she? She doesn't really need you as much as you need her.

And the fact she needed Mandy to combat her own loneliness made her sad, but she was so afraid of being hurt again.

Of being left alone.

Of caring for someone and having it taken away.

It was a scary thing to think of, this thing called love.

Oh, God.

Her heart began to race. She needed to get out of there.

This couldn't be happening to her.

She wouldn't let it.

Henry checked on his burn patient in the intensive care unit. The patient was still intubated because the damage to his lungs was too great to try to wean him off the oxygen, but he was stable enough that Henry was able to work on the extensive burns.

He debrided the burns and dressed them again, a lengthy procedure, but he didn't mind. It was something he often assigned to residents or interns, but they didn't have those here at Aspen Grace Memorial Hospital, which was okay today. It kept his mind off the fact that he had curled up around Kiera. And the fact that he hadn't slept so soundly and so well in a very long time.

He hadn't realized until this morning how much he needed that kind of deep sleep. He had forgotten what it felt like to feel so safe and relaxed with someone. To know that he wasn't alone in the night.

He'd been a little freaked out to wake up and discover the pillow wall gone and Kiera in his arms, like it was the most natural thing in the world for his unconscious body to seek her out for comfort.

And that he liked it.

A lot.

And how he couldn't stop thinking about her bottom pressed against him, the shape of her body and how it fitted so well against him.

He couldn't remember the last time he had slept like that.

Yes, you do. It was when Michelle was alive.

And he realized he hadn't slept that well in eight years. He'd been a zombie for eight years.

"Dr. Baker?"

He looked up from his work to see a nurse hovering in the door.

"Yes?" he asked, going back to his work.

"Your father is in the boardroom and would like to speak with you. He just called down."

Henry sighed, annoyed that his father was back in the hospital and intruding where he didn't belong. His father was obsessed with this new hospital, this new private clinic that his father felt would propel him to the pinnacle to his political career and gain him a lot of votes. And also make him the most money. His father had no real interest in medicine or saving lives. His father was not a doctor—he was a politician, and it all came down to money.

When Henry had been first tasked with coming here, he couldn't have cared less, but now things were different.

"Tell him that I will come and see him once I'm done with my patient."

"Yes, Dr. Baker."

The nurse disappeared and Henry went back to his work.

He knew his father wouldn't be happy that he hadn't jumped and gone to see him straight away, but Henry didn't care.

And his father could wait. His parents didn't care about him. And it was about time he stopped caring for them and moved on with his own life.

All his father's plans for his ridiculously expensive, brand-new private hospital could wait. He really didn't have time for them today.

His father always expected him to jump when he wanted. Henry was not going to jump. Not this time. Even though his father saved him from his reckless life after Michelle died, he shouldn't have to owe his father for that.

No parent should ever blackmail their child.

Henry was tired of being embarrassed about it.

He was tired of hiding behind his mistakes.

Henry finished up his work. He checked the vitals of the patient, wrote up his orders and left the intensive care unit.

He didn't go to see his father; instead, he made his way down to the emerAgency department to find Kiera. The emergency room was quiet. It wasn't full of sick people and he couldn't see Kiera anywhere.

"Have you seen Dr. Brown?" Henry asked a passing triage nurse.

"She's in the free clinic."

"The free clinic is open again?" he asked.

"Yes."

Henry left the emergency room and went through the doors into the free clinic. He spotted some of the hospital's nurse practitioners and Kiera was at the nurses station charting. She looked up and her cheeks flushed pink when their gazes met.

He smiled at her remembering how she'd felt snuggled up against him.

All warm and cuddly.

What has gotten into you?

"Good morning," he said, coming to stand by her.

"Good morning, I'm very glad the free clinic is open. I guess I have you to thank."

"Uh, yeah." Henry was glad the free clinic

was open and that it made Kiera happy. He was shocked that his father had opened it up again. And now he was regretting not going to find out what had changed his father's mind.

"I have to check on a patient out of town and I wondered if you'd like to come with me?"

"Why are you going out of town?"

"It's for an elderly patient. She was one of Dr. Burke's and I've sort of been taking care of her. She's had a rash from her oral chemo, and I thought you might like to join me."

Henry should say no, because being alone with her probably wasn't wise.

He knew how he was feeling about her, but he didn't know how she felt and he really didn't want his heart broken.

Not that it would be her fault. She had made it clear this was simply a business arrangement.

It wasn't her fault he was falling for her.

So he shouldn't spent extra time alone with her, but he didn't want Kiera to go alone.

"I can come with you."

"Good. I was hoping you would, being a plastic surgeon. I thought you might know what to do for her skin irritation. I don't know any dermatologists."

He smiled. She was rambling. It was kind of cute.

"It's fine, Kiera. I can go with you. What time?"

"In three hours?"

He nodded. "Okay. I'll meet you out front in three hours."

"Sounds good." Kiera left to go back to her patients.

Henry took a deep breath. He knew his father would be waiting for him and he didn't care, even though he was curious to know what had caused his father to reopen the clinic. What kind of game was his father playing at?

Whatever it was, Henry didn't want to be involved in it.

Kiera had surprised herself by asking Henry to go with her to see Agnes, who lived two hours out of town and up a windy mountain road, but she had.

It's because he got the free clinic opened again.

Or at least that's what she was telling herself.

That she was so happy the free clinic was open, she had become delusional and invited him. That had to be it. It was a moment of complete weakness.

Liar.

That wasn't the reason. She enjoyed being around him. She had had fun last night. Just like she had had fun at the fundraiser. The night she wore the jade dress and he had kissed her in the car. That hot steamy kiss she still couldn't get out of her mind.

Kiera. You've got to stop this. He's not into you.

She wished he was.

It was nice being around Henry. And she couldn't remember the last time she had had so much fun. She couldn't remember the last time she actually wanted to be with someone again.

To spend time with someone who made her laugh. Someone who turned her on.

Someone who was smart, sexy and talented.

Kiera finished her rounds, changed out of her scrubs and packed what she needed to take for Agnes.

Once her car was loaded she pulled out of the staff parking lot and around to the front of the hospital. Henry had changed out of his scrubs and was dressed in jeans and a suede lambswool Sherpa coat.

Give him a pair of cowboy boots and a baseball cap and he'd fit right in with rural Colorado.

She pulled up and unlocked her door.

"Need a lift?" Kiera teased.

"Sure." Henry opened her back door and tossed his leather messenger bag in the back seat before climbing into the front seat next to her.

"If I didn't know any better, I'd think you were from Colorado."

He grinned at her. "Well, I am from Colorado, but I prefer California. It doesn't snow in California."

"I think it does in some parts of California."

"Not in my part of California. Not Los Angeles, not Huntington Beach, which is where I live."

"Fancy."

"It is. Quite fancy and peaceful." Henry grinned at her. "I love the beach."

"That sounds nice. Do you surf then, living so close to the water?"

"No. No time."

"Then why live at the beach?"

"It's the best, and the sounds of the waves help me sleep."

"Do you have problems sleeping?"

"I do. The sound of the water relaxes me. Sometimes," he said quietly.

"It must be hard for you to sleep in Aspen then. There's no ocean here."

"It is, but I forgot about hearing the wind through the trees, it's almost like waves sometimes. And also… Anyway, I slept well last night. Must've been the warm milk."

She glanced at him briefly. Her heart skipped a beat. She had thought for a second he was going to say he'd slept well last night because of her, because that's how she felt, too.

She had slept so soundly with him beside her. She had been comfortable. She had felt safe. The only other time she'd felt as safe was the first night at Wilfred and Mandy's. Sharing a room with Mandy in a warm, dry, clean, quiet home had given her security.

"The milk would have been better with cinnamon," she said, trying to get her mind off him. Trying to forget his strong arms around her.

"You'll have to make it for me sometime again then, with the correct ingredients."

Kiera's cheeks heated and she turned her focus back on the road.

Maybe this was a bad idea, being alone with Henry for two hours.

At least Agnes would appreciate Henry. She was a feisty eighty-year-old woman who liked a good-looking man.

"So what kind of cancer does... Sorry, I don't know her name."

"Agnes."

"Agnes then. What kind of cancer does Agnes have and what is she taking for it?"

"Lung cancer with metastases to her brain and her bones, mostly her hips."

Henry made a face. "So she's on oral chemo?"

"Yes. She's had radiation for the brain mets. She's been this way for two years."

"Two years, and she's eighty and lives out in the country?" he asked, shocked.

"I know, right? She's pretty hard-core. She was one of Dr. Burke's favorite people."

"I look forward to meeting her."

"I can tell you, you'll make her day."

"Why is that?" he asked.

"She appreciates…" Kiera blushed and cleared her throat. "She likes a…"

"A nice piece of ass?" Henry teased.

Kiera laughed. "Yeah, I guess so."

"You guess so?"

"I haven't seen your…" She couldn't even finish that sentence with a straight face.

"Ass," he said quickly.

"Right. So I wouldn't know."

"Well, we have slept together, and we are engaged."

"A fake engagement," she reminded him. "Fake meaning, I don't see your ass and you don't see mine."

"Ever?" he teased.

Heat bloomed in her cheeks. "Right. Never. Ever."

Instantly she regretted what she had said. How had they gone from talking about their patient to discussing each other's posteriors? What she had to do pay attention to the road.

Nonetheless, she didn't mind talking about his bottom and wouldn't mind seeing it. It would be nice to spend more nights safe in his arms. To feel secure. To trust.

To love.

What has gotten into you?

Kiera kept her eyes on the road and watched for the turnoff to the windy road that headed up the mountain to where Agnes had a small log cabin and lived by subsistence and off-grid.

"Why does she live up here?" Henry asked as they hit a rut and were jostled back and forth.

"She farms, hunts. She likes living off-grid. She always has."

"I'm beginning to like this patient. She's hardcore and appreciates a fine-looking surgeon." He waggled his eyebrows as Kiera glanced at him.

"You know what? I think I liked you better when you were all moody and sullen."

"Thanks… I think."

She chuckled and they pulled up to Agnes's house. There was smoke rising from the stovepipe on the roof, which was always a good sign that Agnes was still alive and kicking.

As Kiera parked the car, the door opened and Agnes stood in the doorway.

"You made it, Doc Brown!" Agnes shouted. "And you've brought a friend!"

"I did. This is Dr. Baker."

Agnes eyed Henry. "Isn't he the governor's son?"

"I am," Henry replied.

"Well, you look fine. Your father is a tool." Agnes turned and headed back into her house. "Come on in."

Kiera laughed silently at Henry's shocked expression.

She might have been regretting her decision to bring him up here because she was scared about how she was feeling, but now she was glad he was there.

Agnes was going to make this trip fun.

So much fun, and for that the drive was completely worth it.

CHAPTER NINE

"So? What's the verdict?" Agnes asked as Kiera finished listening to her chest.

"You're still stable, but I really wish you'd move to town."

Agnes rolled her eyes. "Dr. Burke tried for ten years to get me off my mountain. A little cancer is not going to get me to move to town."

Henry gave Kiera an amused secret look.

"Agnes, I think you're in more pain than you're letting on," she said gently.

"I'm fine. I just have a rash that's annoying me. All over my chest." Agnes glanced at Henry and waggled her eyebrows suggestively. "You want to examine it for me?"

Kiera chuckled silently.

"I can take a look," Henry offered.

Agnes grinned. "So you're really not a politician then?"

"No, politics are only for my—what did you call him?—tool of a father?" Henry teased.

Agnes snorted. "I like him, Doc Brown. I like him. This is the kind of man you should marry!"

Kiera's mouth dropped open and all she could hear was a high-pitched buzz between her ears. An annoying hum, her nervous system trying to drown out the embarrassment of what was happening. What was Agnes insinuating? Had she heard something? Impossible—no one knew. She hadn't even told Mandy.

Warmth bloomed in her cheeks and she hoped she wasn't blushing.

"What?" Kiera asked, clearing her throat as she tried to regain control of her emotions.

"You should go after Dr. Baker here. He's older, hot, and you spend too much time marching for causes. You need to campaign for a piece of Dr. Baker."

"For important issues," Kiera replied.

"I know, Doc Brown, but you're young and you shouldn't be alone. What do you think of her, Dr. Baker?"

"She'll do." Henry grinned.

Kiera groaned inwardly and glared at Henry, who was trying not to laugh as his eyes twinkled.

"Well, I'm trying to get Dr. Brown to marry me. I mean she is my fiancée and all," Henry admitted.

Kiera snapped her mouth shut and glared at Henry, who was enjoying her discomfort.

"Well, that's wonderful, Doc Brown! Burke… Wilfred…your father, that is, would be so proud of you!" Agnes said.

"What're you talking about, Agnes?" Kiera asked.

"Wilfred wanted you and Mandy to be happy. That's all. You know he loved you, don't you?"

The mention of Dr. Burke's name and the association of Dr. Burke as her father struck a nerve with her. It made her emotional.

It was hard to breathe. Hard to swallow. She met Henry's gaze and the mirth was gone. And she knew he could see her pain.

He could see her grief and vulnerability again. She knew how Dr. Burke felt about her. How she had loved him like a father.

How she grieved him still.

What she didn't like was losing control here in front of Henry and Agnes.

"How about I take care of that rash, Agnes?" Henry asked, changing the subject from Dr. Burke, for which she was grateful.

It was hard to think of Wilfred. He would've been happy to see her engaged, but would he have been so happy to learn it was a lie?

She thought it would have disappointed him. It was a bit too much to bear.

She cleaned up her equipment while Henry examined Agnes. She smiled watching him with her. He was so kind and gentle. He had an excellent bedside manner.

He was charming, though it was no surprise since he dealt with a lot of high-profile, elite patients. Still, it was refreshing to see him extending the same courtesy to someone who couldn't pay his exorbitant fees.

"This cream and the dressing I just put on should be applied twice a day," Henry said. "If it worsens, can you call me and I'll come back to check?"

"I have a phone. I might be off the grid, but I have a phone." Agnes took the tube from Henry.

"I'll come back in a week anyway, Agnes," Kiera said, closing her bag. "You're doing well. Try not to overdo it."

"Thank you, Doc Brown and Doc Baker."

They slipped on their jackets and headed outside. It was dark, but the sky was clear. There were stars coming out against the inky black sky.

Kiera breathed in the cold air. It was cleansing.

"Thanks for coming with me tonight," she said, and it was true. She was glad he was here.

"Thanks for inviting me." He reached out and touched her face. The simple brush of his fingers against her cheeks sent a delicious shiver through her. A zing of need.

"Well, we should get back to Aspen." Kiera took a step back away from him, trembling, suddenly afraid.

"Right." He cleared his throat. "Right."

Kiera really wanted to kiss him, but she couldn't risk her heart. It was bad enough this whole thing was fake. She wasn't going to get hurt again. Even though she wanted to take the chance with him, to kiss him one more time, she couldn't.

She was terrified. How could she trust someone she didn't know? She couldn't get hurt again.

She wouldn't be left again.

She took risks all the time saving lives, but right here and now, she couldn't take this risk. She never wanted to take this risk again.

It hurt too much.

The drive back to Aspen was quiet. There wasn't much to say. Kiera was trying to focus on driving and not the turmoil of emotions racing through her. The desire that was consuming her.

She barely recognized herself.

She was losing control.

The wheel began to pull, and the car began

to shudder. There was a loud pop and the car jolted.

"What's happening?" she shouted, gripping the wheel.

"I think you have a flat."

Kiera cursed under her breath and flicked on her hazards. As she did, her engine light came on and there was smoke. Her car sputtered, lurching forward.

"I think it's more than a flat," she murmured.

"I would say so," Henry remarked.

She managed to get over to the shoulder of the road. She was just thankful they were on the main road now, not on Agnes's treacherous, mountain road in the dark. And they weren't at a mountain pass. They were on a flat section of the road though still far out of town.

Once she got over to the side of the road, her car gave one last awful shudder and died.

It gave out with one last great heave.

"Time of death, twenty-one oh-two." Kiera leaned her head against the steering wheel and gently began to bang it.

"Hey, no banging the head against the steering wheel. This is a solvable problem."

She looked at him and picked up her cell phone to call a cab. The moment she touched it, it flicked off and the battery died. "Okay?

My cell is dead because, apparently, I left it in the car on a cold night. How is yours?"

Henry pulled out his phone. "I have batteries, but no reception."

"Great."

"Well, we can't sit here. We have to get to a phone. This might be a main road, but I haven't seen any cars in a bit. However, about half a mile back I saw a restaurant and a motel. We could wait for help there."

"Let's go then."

As much as she didn't want to walk back to that rest stop, she didn't want to spend a bitterly cold night in her car on the side of the road, in the dark with Henry. The last time they had spent time at the side of the road in the dark waiting for a tow truck, they had shared a passionate kiss and she had let down her guard.

It had been a total moment of safety. Of letting go.

A moment of feeling she was free.

And she longed to feel that again.

Only it wasn't a smart idea to do that.

Not tonight, and not with her conflicted feelings. A small diner would be a perfect spot to sit up all night, drink bad coffee and keep warm.

And it was public.

Henry wouldn't try to make out with her in public.

Or would he?

They walked in silence along the side of the road, back toward that diner. Kiera shivered even though she had her winter coat on. The wind had picked up and was blowing down off the mountain. It sent a chill right down her spine and she couldn't wait for a cup of coffee.

"See, I was right," Henry muttered.

"Right about what?"

"California is so much better."

She chuckled through chattering teeth. "Right about now I would have to agree with you."

It was hard to walk along the side of the road, through slush and snow intermixed with chunks of ice. She had to concentrate on not falling over and keeping her footing so that she didn't stumble.

Half a mile, which wasn't that long of a distance, felt like it was all the way to Timbuktu. By the time they got to the diner, she was sweating from exertion and also chilled to the bone.

Henry pulled out his phone. "Still no bars."

"I'm sure the diner will have a phone that we can borrow." She opened the door and welcomed the blast of warm air.

"Grab a seat and I'll see if I can call a tow truck."

Kiera nodded and slid into a booth, trying to get warm again.

Henry made his way to the counter of the almost empty diner and spoke with the waitress. She handed him her phone and Henry made a call.

As Kiera sat there and tried to warm up, she realized she was shaking for another reason.

She avoided places like this.

Honey, how long have you been here? the police officer had asked her gently.

Kiera had shied away. Her father didn't like police officers and had told her they weren't safe. *Dunno.*

Are you waiting for someone?

Daddy.

The police officer had nodded. *Where did he go?*

To the car. He left the money there. She'd brushed away a tear, wishing her father would come back.

Why don't you come with me?

I can't. Daddy could come back.

We'll let him know where to find you if he does.

You swear? Kiera had asked.

The police officer had nodded. *I swear.*

Her reverie was interrupted by a waitress.

"Coffee? You look like you need it," the waitress asked, interrupting the memory Kiera thought was long buried.

"That would be great. And one for my friend."

The waitress nodded and filled the two white mugs that were on the table. "The kitchen is closed, but we can do sandwiches if you're hungry?"

"I'm good for now, but thanks!"

The waitress nodded and walked away as Henry came and slid into the booth, still shivering. "The tow truck will take it into Aspen tomorrow morning and the only rental agency in this town is closed for the night."

"So, there's no way to get back to Aspen?" she asked. She didn't want to stay here. She was uncomfortable. She hated diners.

"Not tonight. I even called Mike, but my father has him for the night. Mike said he can come tomorrow to get us."

Kiera groaned. "Great. Just how I wanted to spend my night, sitting up in a diner. Shivering."

"There is a motel right next door."

The suggestion caught her off guard. Her eyes widened and her heart hammered against her chest.

"What?"

"We're both wet and cold. We can hang our clothes up to dry in our rooms, have a shower and stay warm. And it's not a diner."

Henry was right. The last thing she needed to do was catch a cold. The smart thing was to cut her losses and try and get some sleep tonight. And Henry had said "rooms," although secretly she wouldn't mind sharing a room with him. Of course, since they had left Agnes's she'd been trying not to think about him.

Or kissing him.

Or the need he stirred in her. A motel wouldn't help one bit.

"Rooms, right?" she asked, quickly.

"Of course."

"Okay."

They finished their coffee, paid for some sandwiches and headed through the adjoining doors into the small motel that was attached to the diner.

The owner of the motel looked up from his paper. "How can I help you folks?"

"We were hoping you had a couple of rooms for the night?"

"I only have one room left," the motel manager said.

Kiera's heart started to race. "Only one room?"

"It has two beds," the owner said.

Even though she knew it would be a mistake, they really had no choice and she nodded to Henry, who looked just as worried as she did.

They were adults.

Nothing had to happen.

They could control themselves for one night.

"Okay. We'll take it." Henry paid the motel owner, and once the paperwork was filled out and the owner had handed them keys, they made their way back outside into the cold. Down to the end of the motel where they had the very last room.

As Henry put the key in the door, the sign flicked from Vacancy to No Vacancy.

"I've never seen that happen before."

"I'm sure you don't really stay at retro motels that were popular in the sixties."

"No. That's true." He opened the door and stepped in, flicking on the lights. Kiera followed him and she was relieved to see there were two beds.

The room was clean and completely outdated, but it was a warm and a safe place to be until morning.

She set her bag down on the bed closest to the door and Henry set down the sandwiches and his bag on the small dinette set. He locked the door and pulled the drapes so the streetlights wouldn't shine in on them.

"Do you want to shower first? A hot shower will warm you up faster. Then we can have our dinner." He wasn't looking at her as he peeled off his wet jacket and draped it over a chair.

"Yeah, that would be nice." She was hoping

that her voice wasn't shaking, revealing her anxiety about being alone with him in this room.

Not that *he* would do anything; it was herself she was nervous about.

She honestly didn't know why she was fighting it.

She was an adult.

She'd done this before and she wanted to again and with Henry.

You can't.

Only she really wanted to.

Her skin broke out in goose bumps, and she took off her wet jacket and placed it on the other chair.

"I'll be quick, so I don't use all the hot water."

Henry smiled briefly. "Great."

She nodded and felt her cheeks warm as she scurried to the bathroom. Once she was in there, she was able to lock the door and take a deep breath.

This was going to be a long night.

Henry heard the shower come on and he tried not to think about the fact that only a thin wall separated him from a very naked and wet Kiera. He had to pull himself together. This was not an ideal situation, that was for sure.

He'd rather be in his own room.

But would he really not think about her showering in his condo?

His blood was hot, his body wound tight because he wanted her, and he was holding himself back.

It had been a long time since he'd wanted someone like this.

This was probably a bad idea, but since they were stuck, he could resist for one night. He could make it through to morning.

Henry sat on the edge of his bed, waiting for his turn in the shower. After that he was going to climb into his bed and tie himself down.

Because he was so tempted when it came to Kiera Brown.

So very tempted.

The shower stopped and his pulse was thundering in his ears as he watched the door open and Kiera slip out. A too-short towel was wrapped around her. She'd braided her damp, long red hair.

He kept his gaze focused on her legs as she scooted across the room, pulled back the covers and climbed into her bed, pulling the blankets up to her chin. She was shivering.

"Are you cold?"

"A bit. I didn't realize how much it had affected me," she said through chattering teeth.

Without thinking he left the safety of his own bed and came to sit down on her bed. She didn't move away from him. She just clutched her covers tighter, under her chin.

He reached back to his bed and pulled off the top cover. He wrapped it around behind her, pulling it around her. And then he pulled her close to him, holding her as she shivered. She was so close he could feel her breath on his neck and it sent a curl of desire through him.

He wanted to kiss her again, but when he had touched her face outside Agnes's place, she'd pulled away. Just like with the first kiss they'd shared in the car. She'd pulled away then, too. She didn't want him and that was fine.

Kiera gazed up at him, her mouth open and her green eyes sparkling in the dim light. He keenly remembered the feel of her lips and wanted to taste them again.

"Well," he said, breaking the silence that always seemed to come between them when they were close like this. "I think I'll go have a shower."

"Okay," she whispered, still shivering.

"You're so cold."

"I know. I can't get warm."

Henry glanced at the shower, but he couldn't

leave her shivering like this. So instead he stood up and pulled off his shirt. Her eyes widened.

"What're you doing?"

"My clothes are wet and you're freezing. I'm going to climb into bed with you."

Kiera just nodded. She didn't argue with him, because he was pretty sure she knew the fastest way to regulate temperature was for him to take off his cold, damp clothes and cuddle up close to her.

And that's what he had to focus on.

He was just helping her stay warm. That was it.

He removed his wet socks and slipped off his jeans, keeping on his boxer briefs, so he wouldn't freak her out further. He grabbed the rest of the blankets from the bed and climbed in beside her.

Kiera didn't fight him or make a sarcastic comment. Instead, she snuggled up against him, her head resting against his chest as he held her in the double bed. And he realized she didn't have the towel on anymore and that it was her naked body pressed against him, holding him.

"Your heart is racing," she whispered, her head on his chest.

"Can you blame me?" he said, pulling her closer.

Her shivering stopped and she looked up at him. "No, because my heart is racing, too."

Henry touched her face. "You really are so beautiful."

Pink flushed in her cheeks and she worried her bottom lip. And all he could think about was how soft her lips were. How close she was.

How much he burned for her.

Wanted her.

Needed her.

"About that kiss…"

"We don't need to talk about that kiss." He wanted to do more than talk about that kiss. He wanted to relive it. Right here. Right now.

He yearned to taste her again. Over and over and never let her go.

He needed her out of his mind.

He wanted the lust out of his blood.

"I think we do."

"Why? It was a kiss. You made it very clear to me that you didn't want to kiss me, and that's okay."

"What do you mean?" she asked. "I wanted that kiss, Henry. I liked it."

His blood heated. "You pushed me away, and then tonight, when I touched you, you pulled away again."

Kiera sighed. "It's because I'm terrified. Henry, I've never wanted a man as much as

I want you. You make me feel safe and that scares me."

"Wy does it scare you?"

"Because I can't trust you."

That made him pause. He wanted her to trust him.

"You're safe with me. I promise. I won't hurt you."

She reached up and touched his face and he closed his eyes, reveling in the sensation of her touch, the softness of her skin on his.

He grabbed her hand and instinctively kissed the pulse point of her wrist.

She was scared. So was he.

He'd been with other women since Michelle, but Kiera was the first woman who had made his blood burn with desire. She was the first since Michelle who made him want more.

And that scared him, too.

Kiera sighed as he stroked her arm, touching the bare skin he could.

He wanted her. He wanted to kiss her again. And he pulled her closer, touching her face, making her shiver as he touched her. Her breath coming quickly. He leaned in and drank in the scent of her skin.

Kissing her neck lightly as she sighed. Her blood racing through her neck, under his lips. The blankets that she'd been clutching to her so tightly fell away and he pulled her onto his lap, her long legs going around his waist as he trailed his kisses lower, his hands on her back.

"Henry," she whispered. "Kiss me. This time, I want you to kiss me."

He cupped her face with his hands and captured her lips with his. There was nothing more to say. He wanted her. He had wanted her from the first moment he'd laid eyes on her, when she'd pulled off her ridiculous woolen beanie and scarf after protesting outside.

He had wanted her every time she'd fought with him.

He had wanted her when she made her deal with him, when she came down the stairs in that jade dress.

Every day that he'd known her, he had wanted her.

And it was too much.

He prided himself on his control. Perfectionism, because when things were perfect he didn't have to feel anything.

He didn't want to feel.

He was numb, and it had been okay until Kiera had stumbled into his life.

His tight rein of control was slipping, and he didn't care. Not with her in his arms.

His tongue twining with hers.

He stopped himself, although it was so hard with her naked in bed with him.

"Kiera, I don't want... I don't ever want to hurt you."

And he meant it.

He cared for her. In this short amount of time she'd gotten through all his defenses like no one had done since Michelle.

"You won't," she whispered, her lips hovering over his, her delicate hands cupping his face. "You won't." And she kissed him again.

It was then he knew he was a lost man.

"Be with me tonight, Kiera. Be with me."

"I want that." She kissed him gently. "I want that. This doesn't have to mean anything. I just want to be with you. Feel you."

Henry couldn't argue except that for him it meant something. He took her in his arms, pulling her closer. Touching her like he wanted to.

Just as he had wanted to do when he'd first met her.

It was so good to feel again. It had been so long. He usually just went through the motions. This was different, something he hadn't felt in a long time.

A rush of feelings he couldn't even get a grasp on.

It was like being alive when he'd been dead before.

Awake.

It also felt like a dream, one he didn't want to wake up from.

They sank against the mattress together, kissing. He wanted to taste her, he wanted to be in this moment with her. Inside her. Claiming her.

He wanted Kiera to be his.

The realization jarred him, and he shook the thought from his head.

There was no need to think about this now, or that it scared him.

Right now, in this moment, all he needed was to feel.

Henry tipped her chin till she was looking up at him. Her cheeks were flushed, her lips were swollen from their shared kisses, and her green eyes sparkled in the dim light.

"You're beautiful." He kissed her again, his lips urgent as he pulled her flush with him. He didn't want an ounce of space between them.

He let his mouth tail down from her lips, down her neck and over her breasts, kissing each one of her pulse points.

Tasting all he could of her.

He was hungry.

"Henry, I want you so much," she murmured.

"I want you, too." And admitting that made him feel free. His life since Michelle had died had been about control.

Numbness.

Control so he didn't succumb to grief.

He didn't feel. There was no point to living.

With her in his arms and her wanting him, he felt free. Like something had sparked anew in him. He was alive.

"Do you have protection?" she asked.

"I do." And he was thankful he carried it with him always.

He shifted away, not wanting to leave the warmth of her embrace, to grab protection out of his leather messenger bag. He got what he needed and put it on. He returned to her and resumed kissing her all over, touching her, making her tremble under his touch.

She was hot and wet for him between her thighs.

"I want you," she panted, wrapping her legs around him, urging him to take her.

He was more than happy to oblige. Her pleas were all he needed as he settled between her legs and slowly entered her. Possessing her. She fit so tight around him.

Hot and warm.

It was almost more than he could take. She moved her hips, urging him deeper, to take her harder and faster.

She was so warm.

So tight.

He couldn't hold back as he moved in and out of her. Thrusting into her hot depths.

It was just the two of them, locked together, gazing into each other's eyes as they moved in sync. He ran his hands over her, reveling in the softness of her skin. He slipped his hand under her bottom, cupping her leg, holding her tight against him as he took her.

Just as she took him.

She wanted him as much as he wanted her.

It wasn't long before she squeezed him, gasping and crying out, her nails digging into his back as she came around him. It wasn't long before he followed.

Giving in to the pleasure.

He rolled over onto his back and she curled up against him, resting her head on his chest. Henry held her close, not wanting to let her go.

He had never thought it would be like this. He'd never thought he'd ever feel like this again.

When he was with her, he lost all control.

It frightened him, because he didn't know anything else besides control and grief.

It had been a long time since he'd felt anything close to love.

And that was terrifying.

CHAPTER TEN

KIERA DIDN'T KNOW when she fell asleep, but she slept soundly after making love with Henry. She'd been with other men, but nothing compared to this. Nothing had ever felt like this before.

She'd never before experienced this kind of pleasure with someone.

All consuming.

It had burned her blood until she'd erupted into a ball of flames, melting in his arms. At first, when he had taken her in his arms when she was cold, she had felt exposed and vulnerable, but he had made her feel safe.

And it just felt right.

She didn't feel afraid.

She felt she could be herself and she wasn't embarrassed. Kiera let herself go. She wanted him and she wasn't scared to tell him that. She'd wanted him from the first moment she saw him, and even though she was trying so hard to deny it she couldn't.

With his arms around her, she'd just let go.

She wanted to taste his lips.

She wanted to taste his passion.

She didn't regret her decision to give in last night, but now, in the light of day, she didn't know what she was feeling. She wanted to stay with him, but he didn't live in Aspen, and after the issues with the new hospital and Aspen Grace Memorial Hospital were taken care of, he was going to leave.

Henry had a practice, a home, a life in Los Angeles.

And Kiera was needed here in Aspen. She couldn't leave.

The last time she had been away, Mandy was hurt, and Wilfred had fought his cancer alone.

He'd died alone.

She couldn't leave.

Why? What is holding you here?

This was where her home was because this was where Mandy was. Mandy was her only family and vice versa. Keira couldn't leave her all alone.

Not after all Dr. Burke had done for her, all that Mandy had done to support her.

Where would her life be if Dr. Burke hadn't

taken her in and raised her as his own? Kiera shuddered as she thought of that diner in Colorado Springs, of how alone she'd felt sitting there, watching at the window for her father to come back for her.

The flashing lights of the police cruiser, and going with the nice police officer to her first temporary foster home.

She remembered finally standing in front of Dr. Burke's house. She'd been scared, but his smile and the feel of his strong hand as he took her in and introduced her to Mandy had reassured her. That was when she had felt safe, she had felt at home. When Wilfred died and Brent left her for another woman she felt like that little abandoned girl again. Now, here with Henry, she felt the same safety and security. Still, she couldn't leave Aspen. She'd left once before and that had turned out bad. She couldn't leave again. This was the only place in her life that had ever been good. And any future with Henry was uncertain.

It was scary to even entertain the thought of leaving.

It was too great of a risk.

She couldn't leave Mandy behind. It hurt her heart to know that this fling with Henry was just that and it was temporary.

Soon he'd be gone and she'd feel…empty.

She owed it to Dr. Burke and Mandy to stay here.

Kiera sighed and got up as quietly as she could.

"You're disappearing on me again?" Henry asked groggily.

Kiera smiled and sat back down. "I didn't want to disturb you."

He reached out and touched her face. "Well, at least this time you have nowhere to go and I didn't find you struggling at the foot of the bed."

She laughed. "This is true."

He grinned lazily and pulled her back down onto the bed. "What's your rush?"

Kiera kissed him. "Mike is coming soon. I want to be ready."

Henry frowned and groaned. "Right."

"You sound so disappointed."

He scrubbed a hand over his face. "I'm sure Mike will tell me how angry my father is with me."

"Why would your father be angry with you? It was my car that broke down."

"Because my father wanted to meet with me yesterday. He summoned me when I was in the intensive care unit tending to our burn victim.

Instead, I came down to the emergency room and we went to see Agnes."

"Oh." Kiera's stomach flip-flopped. "I wonder if it had to do with the hospital."

"Probably, but he opened the free clinic."

Kiera sat up straighter. "Yeah, but he still wants to close down Aspen Grace Memorial. He still wants to build a new hospital."

"Aspen Grace Memorial is outdated and falling apart. It would cost more to expand and fix what's broken than to build new."

She had a bad feeling. "I think you should have gone to see him."

Henry took her hand. "My father pulls this kind of stuff all the time. Expects me to be at his beck and call, and it's usually nothing."

"Why do you whatever he asks then?"

Henry sighed. "When Michelle died my life was a mess. I abandoned patients, almost lost my medical license because of it. I drank. I gambled. I was on a collision course to destroy my life. My father didn't want to ruin his career with a black sheep of a son, so he set me back on the right path. Hushed everything up, and I worked hard to sober up and save my career."

"Sounds like he cares."

Henry snorted. "Hardly."

"Someone who cares would help."

"He says I owe him. He brings up my past all the time to control me. Soon I'll be free though."

"What's that supposed to mean?" she asked, her stomach anxiously twisting.

"Nothing. Look, he wouldn't do anything drastic without one of the majority shareholders there. Don't worry."

"I thought you weren't the chairman anymore?"

"I'm not, but I still have shares and the right to vote."

"Right." She nodded, but something was wrong. Her insides were in knots and it just didn't feel right.

She didn't trust Governor Baker. Not for a second. The man cared only about money, and she wouldn't put it past him to do something dubious. And now that she was learning how he treated his own son, it felt even more wrong.

Something was going on.

She worried that Henry was hiding more from her.

Kiera didn't doubt that he would do something underhanded, something sneaky. Henry had promised her that if she went along with his ruse he'd save the free clinic and see what he could do the rest, but what if Henry was like his father?

She didn't know him.

You're being paranoid. Henry is nothing like that.

She hated her sense of dread. Anxiety was eating away at her because she couldn't trust Henry not to hurt her. She couldn't trust anyone.

She was annoyed at herself for a fleeting second for entertaining something more with Henry. She had let go of the tight hold on her emotions and fallen into his arms.

"Are you okay, Kiera?" Henry asked.

"Fine." And she plastered on a fake smile. "I'm going to get dressed and ready for Mike to make an appearance."

"Good idea."

Kiera wrapped one of the tangled sheets around her body and scooted to the safety of the bathroom to get dressed.

She couldn't think clearly when she was in the same room as Henry. Having him naked in the bed, she was tempted to ignore the rational part of her that was telling her to be careful and not to trust him and instead listen to the part of her that craved his touch.

She cursed under her breath, unable to remember the last time she'd been so at war with herself.

Focus.

Kiera finished getting cleaned up and changed

in the bathroom. As she left the bathroom Henry stood up, completely naked, and came over to her.

Her pulse was thundering in her ears as she stood there and stared at him. Her body thrummed with lust because, even though she was fighting her feelings, she was completely attracted to him.

Henry pulled her into his arms and kissed her again, pulling her flush against his hard body and giving her a kiss that made her melt.

Kiera didn't want to end the kiss, but she needed to if she was going to keep her sanity and her wits about her.

She pushed him away playfully. "You need to get ready."

He grinned, his eyes twinkling. "Fine."

She watched him head to the bathroom with his clothes. She closed her eyes, taking a deep breath.

She hoped she was wrong. She had to believe she was wrong about Henry. She was worrying too much, and she hated she couldn't let herself trust him.

She hated herself for being so afraid.

Something had changed about Kiera, and Henry couldn't quite put his finger on it. It worried him, especially after telling her about his past.

About the mess he'd made of his life, but he was tired of hiding behind it. He was tired of being abandoned and it didn't bother him to tell Kiera. She was different from the women he dated in Los Angeles.

She was real.

Not vapid. Not shallow.

She was genuine, and that's what drew him.

For the first time, he wished that this wasn't a fake engagement. He liked being around her and he wanted her to come with him to California. He didn't want to leave her behind in Aspen when his time was up. He hadn't realized how lonely he was. Being with Kiera reminded him of what he'd been missing.

He just wasn't sure she felt the same or that she would leave.

You don't know unless you ask her.

That made him nervous and being nervous around her annoyed him. Kiera was getting under his skin, just like Michelle had, and he felt a pang of guilt for even contemplating moving on from Michelle's memory.

She's been gone eight years, and she'd want you to move on.

This was true, but was he ready to move on?

Henry sighed and finished up in the bathroom. When he left, Kiera had opened the drapes and was staring outside.

"Any sign of Mike?" he asked.

She glanced back. "No. Hopefully soon. I hope the tow truck gets my poor old car back to Aspen. Not that it's old."

"It will. Do you want Mike to take you back to your home or the hospital?"

"Home," Kiera said. "I have to check on Mandy. I'm sure she's worried sick."

"I called her from the diner and let her know."

Her eyes widened in surprise. "You did?"

"I didn't want her to worry, and I know you didn't want her to sit up all night."

She smiled sweetly. "Thank you. I meant to call her, but I forgot."

"My pleasure, and I'm sorry I forgot to mention it last night, too." He came up behind her and resisted the urge to wrap his arms around her and hold her. That's what he wanted to do, but he didn't.

He hadn't intended for last night to happen, but he was so glad that it had.

He had wanted it to happen.

A familiar car pulled into the parking lot.

"There's Mike," he said.

"I'll go return the key," Kiera said quickly, grabbing her stuff. "I'll see you in a few minutes."

"Okay."

Kiera slipped out of the motel room. Henry

packed up the rest of his stuff and left the room. Mike parked the car and got out to open the back door for him.

"You're in hot water," Mike announced.

Henry rolled his eyes. "I'm forty. I don't really care if I'm in trouble with my father."

He was done. He didn't care if the whole world knew about his past.

He was tired of hiding.

He was tired of feeling he owed his father.

He was tired of hoping his father loved him, because his father never would and Henry had made mistakes. Mistakes he was ready to own.

"You might care about this." Mike took his messenger bag to put it in the trunk. "The board voted to have your shares revoked, back to your father. They appointed a new chair and the vote happened."

Henry's stomach sank like a rock. Right down to the soles of his feet. "What do you mean the vote happened?"

"They voted without you. The free clinic is gone. All emergency patients are being rerouted and Aspen Grace Memorial Hospital has been closed. They're not even going to build a replacement hospital. The new clinic is going to be for plastic surgery and other spa-like medical treatments. The entire staff have lost their jobs. Or they will when the hospital actually closes.

Only the surgeons have been given severance packages."

"And this happened last night?"

"Your father was pretty angry that you didn't come and see him."

"How could he do that, though? He wouldn't do that, the press would be too bad."

"Yeah, but he didn't. Not really, because he appointed a new chairman of the board who made all the cuts. Someone who wasn't related to him. It doesn't look bad for him. He can spin it the right way since he's not the one who made the final decision. He might have been the executioner for Aspen Grace Memorial, but he didn't make the final blow."

Henry scrubbed a hand over his face. His blood was boiling and he glared at his phone, his stupid phone that couldn't even get reception.

How could his father do this?

Aspen Grace Memorial Hospital wasn't the only hospital in Aspen, but it was the foremost trauma center in the area. And the other hospital in Aspen couldn't employ that many people. So many people had lost their jobs. All for what? Because Henry hadn't jumped when his father called for him to come see him? Because he didn't announce his engagement or do what his father wanted and when?

Free clinics did cost a lot, but really he couldn't even give it a week?

What was the point of opening it for twenty-four hours? What was the point of sending him here?

Kiera was out of a job.

She's talented. She'd get another job somewhere else.

She could come to California with him. He would take her to California in a heartbeat.

"Don't say a word of this to Dr. Brown. I'll tell her myself."

Mike nodded. "I promise. I thought you'd want to know what you were walking into. Personally, I think it was a crummy thing to do all around."

Henry smiled at Mike. "It is."

Mike nodded in understanding as Kiera came out of the office.

"Hi, Mike," she said brightly.

"Good morning, Dr. Brown." Mike took her bags and put them in the trunk.

Henry opened the car door for her, and she climbed into the back. He followed and Mike shut their door before climbing into the front seat. The privacy barrier was up.

And Henry was glad for it.

He was reeling while he struggled to figure out what to say. It was going to crush her, and he felt like he'd betrayed her. He felt like he was some kind of villain who had seduced her and then crushed her dreams all in one swoop. He had meant to sell his shares and tell his father he was done, but his father had wrecked that.

He didn't know how to explain this now.

And he was so angry with his father.

Mike drove away from the motel. From that room where it had happened and where for a brief moment in time he got to be in her presence. It was just the two of them. Together.

Vulnerable.

There was no hospital, no past.

It was just them. Together.

They weren't enemies, they hadn't made a deal with one another.

He wanted to be back in that room, back her in arms. He just wanted her.

"Come to California with me."

Kiera's eyes widened in shock. "What?"

"I want you to come to California."

She chuckled. "I don't think so. What's gotten into you?"

"I don't know," he muttered, but he knew exactly what had gotten into him. What he didn't know was how to tell her the truth.

That he'd blown it.

He'd panicked and acted impulsively, and now he had Kiera on edge.

"The offer was sweet," she said, breaking the silence. "I can't leave Colorado."

"Because of your job?"

"Yes, but… Mandy is here. This is her home. I can't leave."

"Do you want to?"

"This is a very strange string of questions."

"Is it? We are engaged." He was trying to keep it light and having a hard time.

Kiera looked at him like he was crazy. "It's fake."

"Is it?" he asked, because he felt like what had happened between them wasn't fake.

A blush colored her cheeks. "I honestly don't know."

And it stung to hear her say that.

What were you expecting?

He didn't know.

"Right. You're right."

Her expression changed. "What's wrong? What's happened?"

Henry sighed. "So about that meeting I was supposed to go to yesterday."

"Right. The meeting. I remember."

"I thought it was my father just wanting me to do his bidding. Only…"

"Only?" Kiera asked. "Only what?"

"Only there was a vote and I was removed from voting."

"Removed? I don't understand," she asked.

"My father decided to be my proxy, since he bought my shares. He took over my shares and voted on the future of Aspen Grace Memorial Hospital."

"And?" Her voice was very quiet.

"Aspen Grace Memorial Hospital is going to be closed."

"And the free clinic?" she asked, her voice tight.

"It's gone."

"What?"

Mike pulled up in front of Kiera's home and parked.

"Kiera, it was shut down. And instead of a new hospital being built, they're going to be building a private clinic that focuses on plastic surgery and medical spa-like treatments."

"Plastic surgery?" There was an accusatory tone in her voice.

"Yes."

"Well, isn't that convenient."

"What?"

"You missed the vote and…" She shook her head. "What's happening to all the staff?"

"Laid off. Except the surgeons get a severance package."

"I see," she said calmly. She glanced out the window.

"Kiera…"

"No. No. You broke your end of the bargain."

"I said I would see what I could do when we made this deal. I wasn't there, and if I had been, I would have put a stop to it. I would've fought."

"Sure."

"Kiera, I was sent here to put a stop to your protesting."

Her blush deepened. "Well, you did that."

"No. I didn't. I was going to sell my shares, but to someone who saw the value in Aspen Grace Memorial Hospital. Someone who would stand up to my father and help. I wanted to be done with him."

Kiera didn't say anything.

"You don't believe me, do you?"

"Why should I?" Kiera asked. "It just seems too convenient."

"What do you mean?" he asked.

"Plastic surgery. Your specialty. So you're going to extend your practice here then? And selling shares? That seems noble enough, but why didn't you tell me this before?"

"What are you talking about?"

Now he was angry. He felt bad this had happened, but it wasn't his fault. Why couldn't she see that? He hadn't wanted this, and there was nothing convenient about this situation.

"You're a plastic surgeon. Your clients come here, all the elite do."

"So? I don't want to live in Colorado. I don't want to be here. My home is in California. I won't be working at this private clinic."

The way she reeled back, it was as if he had slapped her across the face, as if he'd hurt her, and that was the last thing he ever wanted to do. He would never want to hurt her. He had come here to deal with her; instead, he'd fallen in love.

"Is this why you asked me to move to California?" she asked, her voice catching. "Because you knew I would be fired?"

"I want you, Kiera."

She shook her head. "What we have isn't real."

And that hurt him. "So you only slept with me because of our deal?" He hated saying it, but he was hurt and had lost control.

He was angry with his father. He was mad at himself. All he wanted was her.

His heart ached because he was falling in love with Kiera. He'd known that since the first night they had spent together, with that ridiculous pillow wall between them. Apparently, though, he was the only one feeling these emotions. He'd put his heart on the line and she'd crushed it.

Why had he let her through his barriers?
Because you're lonely.

"How dare you insinuate that! You know that I can't leave Colorado."

"Why?"

"Because we're strangers, because what we have isn't real…"

"It was real enough last night, Kiera. Or did you feel anything?"

Because he wasn't sure. He had certainly felt something. Last night he'd come alive again, and he hadn't realized how long he'd been asleep. Henry was putting a lot on the line here and was scared at what he was doing, but he was learning that life was too short not take a risk. And after last night, he wanted to take that risk with Kiera.

He just wanted Kiera.

All of her. He wrestled with his guilt and his need for her.

He wanted her in California with him because he couldn't be here in Colorado. He couldn't be where Michelle had died, where his parents still lived. He couldn't live this life here. There were too many bad memories. He wanted to start somewhere new with her. It didn't have to be California.

They had both been through a lot of heartache and trauma here.

To move forward he wanted to put this state behind him and never look back.

He wanted to run away with Kiera.

He didn't want to leave her behind, because he felt what had happened to Aspen Grace Memorial Hospital was his fault. He was the one who had cost Kiera her job and he wanted to take care of her, even though she was capable of taking care of herself.

She worried her bottom lip and shook her head. "No. No. I can't leave Mandy. I can't leave Mandy."

"Mandy is a grown woman. You can leave her. She's just an excuse to hold you back from living."

"You know nothing of my life. Nothing," she snapped.

"I know that you're too afraid to leave. You're either feeling guilty because you weren't here when Dr. Burke died or you've been waiting for your father to come back. He won't come back, but, Kiera, you don't have anything tying you down now. You can come to California."

Tears slipped out of her eyes and rolled down her cheek. She brushed them away quickly.

"I can't come to California. You just don't want to be alone. You just feel bad for me. You were using me to get out of a deal with your father."

"That's not it at all."

"No. I can't leave Colorado."

"You're afraid," he snapped. "You're afraid to leave Mandy. Why are you so afraid?"

"Why are you so afraid to make Colorado work? You run from things, Henry. So no, I'm not coming to California with you. I won't run after someone who is always leaving. You broke your promise to me and now I have to leave. I have work to do and a clinic to save. Just stay away from me."

Kiera climbed out of the car and grabbed her bag from Mike.

Henry just sat there.

Angry with himself. Angry that she walked away, but also angry with his father.

Blindingly angry with his father.

Controlling his life again.

And it was going to stop.

CHAPTER ELEVEN

KIERA WAS STRUGGLING to fight back tears as she opened the door to the house. She slammed it shut and leaned against it, closing her eyes and shaking. She was distraught that Aspen Grace Memorial was shutting down, but she was angry with herself because she was more upset about the fact that she had turned down Henry's offer.

That she had said no to California and to him, because part of her wanted to go.

Only she couldn't leave Colorado. Maybe he was right. Maybe she was waiting still.

Maybe emotionally she'd never left that diner.

Mandy was here, but there was a part of her deep down that clung to Aspen and Colorado. She was waiting for her father to come back, even though he never would. Her mother was dead, her dad in prison and Wilfred, he was dead, too. No one was coming for her.

Still, she couldn't leave her family. She couldn't leave Mandy alone.

Loneliness hurt, and she wouldn't put Mandy through that kind of pain.

And that realization had hit too close to home.

She was angry with herself, but she could live with herself if it meant she was taking care of Mandy, because it was Mandy who needed her.

Does she?

Mandy had Derek. How long would she really need her?

She was afraid.

Afraid of getting hurt.

Afraid of being alone.

"Kiera?" Mandy called out.

"I'm home."

Mandy wheeled out of her bedroom with Sif in her lap. "Oh, thank goodness, I was just about to call the state troopers. Especially when I was told your car had been seen being towed into the shop. I even called Agnes and she said you'd left."

"The car died on the way back and my cell was dead, but I thought Henry called you?"

Or did he lie about that, too?

He hadn't told her about his past or the fact his father had sent him here to deal with her. What if he'd just slept with her to distract her.

Well, it had worked.

"Henry called me, but I was still worried. I'm

glad you're okay." Mandy cocked her head to one side. "Are you okay?"

Kiera broke down. "No. I'm not okay."

She made her way to the couch and sat down, and that's when the floodgates opened. She couldn't hold it back any longer. It just came out of her. Emotions she hadn't realized she'd been holding back, since Dr. Burke had died and since she'd been left alone in the diner. Emotions she had kept in check for so long because she never wanted to seem ungrateful for the second chance she'd been given when Wilfred took her into his home. She realized she'd forgotten how to feel. She'd been so busy trying to be happy, to be grateful, that she wasn't really feeling.

"What happened?" Mandy asked gently.

"We were engaged. Henry and I."

Mandy's eyes widened. "Engaged?"

Kiera nodded. "It was fake. Or I thought it was."

"It's not?" Mandy asked, confused.

"We spent last night together."

"Oh!" Mandy smiled. "What's wrong with that then?"

"Henry wants me to go to California with him."

"Why don't you?"

"How can I leave?"

"How can you not? This is your chance at love. Take it."

"Love?" Kiera asked numbly.

"Isn't it? You spent last night together, and I saw the way you two looked at each other. It's pretty obvious," Mandy said.

"Yes. I think I'm in love with him."

"I know! It's great," Mandy said, smiling.

"No. It's not. The board shut down Aspen Grace Memorial Hospital. There was some kind of coup with the board and the shareholders. Henry didn't get a chance to vote. The hospital was shut down, and the free clinic is gone."

"What're they going to build in its place?"

"Some kind of private plastic surgery clinic. One that caters to the rich. Face-lifts and Botox. Peels. Who knows?"

"I see."

"I lost my job."

Sif leaped down from Mandy's lap and clambered up into hers. Kiera stroked the ginger cat lovingly. Sif's moods were usually erratic, but it seemed that Sif knew she shouldn't be a crazy banana pants right now.

That Kiera needed to pet her. It was nice.

"And Henry is going back to California, I take it?" Mandy asked. "Without you?"

Kiera nodded. "He wanted me to go with him. I said no."

"Why? I mean, I thought the whole engagement thing was fast and surprising, but…"

"It was a fake engagement. He told his parents we were engaged to get them off his back, and in exchange he was going to protect the clinic for me. Then the coup happened, and the clinic didn't survive the cut."

Mandy rubbed her temples. "Okay, so let me get this straight, you guys were fake engaged. So in essence you both were sort of using each other to get something, but then you fell in love with him and he fell in love with you, and now neither of you is happy."

"He doesn't love me."

"He invited you to California. I would say he cares about you."

Kiera shook her head. "He doesn't love me."

"Why? Because he didn't keep his end of the bargain?"

"No."

"Then what?"

"I'm afraid. What if…" Kiera trailed off, unable to finish the sentence.

"He cheats on you like Brent cheated on you?"

Kiera sighed. "Yes…"

"He won't."

"Still… I…"

"Then what? Why did you turn him down?

Are you feeling guilty about the hospital and the clinic? Don't… Don't feel guilty about that. There are other good clinics around. You might have to leave Aspen, but there are other towns close by. You did a lot for this community. There's nothing to feel guilty about. Go with him."

"I can't."

"Because you said no?" Mandy asked. "I don't think he'll care if you change your mind."

"Mandy, how I can leave you?" Kiera brushed the tears away. "After all you and your dad did for me? How can I leave Colorado? I've never been able to leave Colorado."

"Yeah, because you're waiting for your family to come back? They're not coming back."

"I know that." A tear slid down her cheek. "I know that now. And how foolish is that of me? I've been sitting around here waiting for them to come back, feeling like that little girl in the diner when you and your father were my family."

"Exactly. He loved you." Mandy reached out and took her hand. "I'm always here. I won't leave you. Wherever we go, we're family."

"I loved him. And he left, too. I can't leave you. I left you once and…"

"You are not the reason for my accident. Don't you ever feel guilty about that. I've made my peace with what happened, and all the work you've done has been admirable, but I never asked that of you. Kiera, I'm fine. I'm okay."

"No. Mandy… I don't want you to be alone."

Mandy took Kiera's hand. "I'm not alone, Kiera. That's what I'm trying to say to you. Derek and I are getting married. He proposed and I accepted."

Kiera's mouth dropped open. "You're getting married?"

Mandy nodded. "Yes. I'm happy, Kiera. I love having you here in my life, and you're welcome to stay forever. You're my sister. I love you, but don't put your life on hold anymore. Not for the family that abandoned you and certainly not for me."

Kiera began to sob when the realization hit her that she *had* been putting her life on hold. She did the things she did because she was just *paused*. How long had she been doing that?

Waiting for people to come back as an excuse to keep everyone away.

And it hurt, because it was Mandy she clung to. She was so alone, but with Henry she felt alive.

It was scary to feel. To be alive.

She'd spent so many years, just frozen. Waiting.

And she didn't know what for. Her biological parents were never coming back. Dr. Burke was dead. Mandy had Derek. Mandy had found love and was happy. Kiera had no one, but she could if she would take a leap of faith.

Mandy didn't need her, and Kiera had been using Mandy as an excuse because she was so afraid of opening her heart, of letting someone in, of losing someone again. She was afraid of being left behind.

"I love you, Kiera. I will admit that I'll hate it if you move to California, but I want you to be as happy as I am with Derek, and if Henry Baker is that person for you, you have to take the chance. Live your life!"

Kiera nodded. "I think I blew it with him."

Mandy smiled. "I doubt that very much. Go, find him. Make things right."

Kiera pulled Mandy into a hug, holding her tight. "I love you."

"I know. I love you, too. Go. Be happy, that's all our dad wanted. He wanted you to be happy and he would be proud of you for working and fighting so hard for the free clinic, but he also knew what love was with my mom. And he wanted that for you. He wanted that for both of us. So, go claim it."

Kiera nodded. Sif jumped down off her lap and scampered away like a bat out of hell, which was Sif's usual behavior around Kiera.

"I'll be back."

Mandy nodded. "I want to hear all about it later."

Kiera grabbed her purse and headed out the door. She didn't have a car, but Aspen Grace Memorial Hospital wasn't far from her place. And she hoped that Henry had gone there first to confront his father.

She hoped that he wasn't getting on a plane for California.

At least, not without her.

"You closed the free clinic?" Henry shouted as he slammed the door of the boardroom behind him.

Henry's father looked up from the paperwork he was doing at the table. "It bled money. It made sense fiscally to do that. Maybe if you had been here to vote…"

"Voting by proxy takes into account what the absentee voter wants. You didn't take that into account."

"I thought I did," his father said.

"Don't give me that bullshit, Father. Your lackeys might eat that up, but I'm not one of your lackeys. Even though you want me to be."

His father's lips formed a thin line and Henry knew that he'd pissed him off.

Good.

He wanted to pick a fight with someone. He was crushed that Kiera had been so hurt and blamed him.

And Henry was angry with himself for putting himself out there only to be rejected. That his heart, was once more the object of pain.

He was furious that his father had sent him to Aspen and put him in this situation. And he was mad with himself for allowing it all these years.

His father would never change.

And he was tired of trying to please his parents for love they couldn't give.

He was done.

And he wanted to fight.

"Well, I'm sorry that I didn't understand your wishes, but Henry, you didn't seem to understand mine when I asked you to come to Aspen and deal with the Dr. Brown situation. Instead, you brought her to one of my fundraisers, where she spent the whole evening chatting up investors who were more than happy to invest in the free clinic. And then I find out you're engaged to her. And you couldn't even announce it like I asked. You had to sneak around."

Henry was confused. "So are you telling me that the free clinic has money?"

"Yes the free clinic has money, but that's not the point. The point is you were supposed to come into Aspen and you were supposed to stop her from her ridiculous protesting and shut the free clinic and the hospital down. You owe me this."

"I owe you nothing. You're just mad she ruined your plans."

His father's eyes narrowed. "A free clinic in the medical facility we have planned will attract the wrong kind of people."

Henry shook his head. "And your son getting married to someone like Dr. Brown sends the wrong message."

"I put up with Michelle because, at the very least, she wasn't an abandoned child of drug addicts. Did Dr. Brown tell you that? Did she tell you that she was left at the side of the road at a diner. Her mother died of an overdose in a dingy Montana slum hospital and her father is serving time for selling drugs. She's the child of meth heads."

"She saves lives!" Henry shouted. "And those people may have biologically brought her into this world, but she is not their daughter. She's Dr. Wilfred Burke's daughter and he was a well-respected and well-liked physician in Aspen. Kiera is nothing like the people who gave birth to her. She's better than that. She's a healer. And so am I."

"You do face-lifts." His father rolled his eyes. "It's done. There's no changing the board now."

"It's not going to look so good to all those people who gave money to the free clinic now, is it?" Henry warned. "You're building a spa now instead of a hospital with a free clinic. That looks bad."

His father's back stiffened. "You wouldn't?"

"No. You're right. I wouldn't, but I can sever ties with you and Mother. How would that look to your potential voters? Won't they question why the beloved son of Governor Baker has cut ties with his family? Especially since you seem to spout off that family ties are so important and that we're all so close. Maybe your voters would like to know that you sent me off to boarding school and that you chased away the woman I fell in love with because she was abandoned as a child."

"You wouldn't." His father stood up. "You wouldn't dare do that to me. Not after all I've done for you!"

"What have you done for me? You paid for my education—well, I can pay that back. You put me on the boards of hospitals in Colorado, but I can see that it was to protect your own assets. I am thankful for you helping me out after Michelle died, but enough. I owe you nothing. I don't care if it ruins me. I'm done with you."

"You're done with me?" his father shouted. "You're ungrateful, after everything I've done."

"For what? The only thing I'm grateful for is that you taught me what kind of man I never want to become." Henry turned on his heel and left.

It felt good to tell his father off.

It was a relief to let that all go, even though he knew that it really wouldn't help. His father wouldn't change and Kiera wouldn't change her mind about him.

He'd put his heart on the line and it was broken again, but he'd taken away something. He'd been so afraid of opening his heart again because of what had happened with Michelle and how her death had almost killed him, but he was lonely, and Kiera had made him feel alive again.

So, even though he didn't have her, Henry felt like he had won.

He just wished that he could have Kiera, too.

He was still in love with her.

He loved her.

And he wanted to marry her, but he'd ruined that. From the moment he'd made a deal with her, he'd ruined that.

He pushed people away because he was so afraid of being alone.

And he had no one to blame but himself.

As he walked down the empty halls of Aspen Grace Memorial Hospital, he tried to shake Kiera from his mind, but he couldn't.

He needed to make things right.

He needed Kiera in his life. He wouldn't give up on her. He wouldn't abandon her.

Even if it meant he had to give up his practice and his beach house, he couldn't live without Kiera.

"Henry!"

He turned around to find his father calling him. "What?"

"Come back. Just please come back and let's talk about this more."

"What more is there to say, Father?"

"Just. Please," his father begged quietly.

Henry nodded and headed back into the boardroom.

"Fine," his father said.

"Fine what?" Henry asked.

"We'll put a free clinic into the new medical facility. It's won't be a hospital, but there will be a clinic. There's enough money to hire back some of the staff from Aspen Grace Memorial. We'll have an emergency free clinic available, and we can work with the other hospital in town for patients."

"You came up with that idea fast."

"It's what was suggested at the board meeting that you missed, but you're right. I turned it down and appointed someone as chairman who would vote the way I wanted."

"You performed a coup, Father. Don't sugar-coat it. I'm not a child."

His father nodded. "You can tell your fiancée that her clinic is saved, but Aspen Grace is in disrepair and it would cost too much to retrofit it and expand."

"I understand."

"I will make the calls to the appropriate staff. I just ask that you don't sever ties with us publicly. And don't sever the ties with your mother. In her own way she does care for you. It would... It would break her heart if you did that."

"I doubt that. She didn't have much time for me."

His father sighed. "That was my fault. She cares for you. She does. Please don't hurt her."

It touched Henry to hear his father talk so softly about his wife. It surprised Henry.

Maybe his father wasn't made of stone.

And Henry wasn't, either.

Henry nodded. "Thank you."

"You're welcome. I do care for you, Henry. I know we sent you off to boarding school, but that's...that's what I knew. It was how I was raised and... I'm sorry if I hurt you. I was wrong, but this is all I know how to give. I don't want you out of my life. I didn't want this to come to blows like this. I'm sorry for holding your mistakes over you."

Henry nodded. "And I hope that you understand that the way I am is all I can give right now to you, as well, but I am willing to try. You did the right thing here today, Father. You bit the bullet and it's a good thing. Keeping the clinic open is the right thing."

"I can't hire back Dr. Brown though."

"Why?" Henry asked.

"It would seem like nepotism in my election year. So I do apologize about that."

"Father, she's not really my fiancée. I persuaded her to pretend to be my fiancée to annoy you, and it worked."

His father smiled. "Is that so?"

"Well, I guess the apple doesn't fall too far from the tree, does it?"

"Then, offer her her job back. If you're not getting married to her, then please announce that so it doesn't look like nepotism."

"I will." Henry went to open the door.

"I do find it strange, though."

"What?" Henry asked, pausing with his hand on the door handle.

"I could've sworn that you two were in love. The way you two looked at each other during the fundraiser. The way I saw you look at her here in the halls of the hospital. And from what

I saw in the papers when you two were at that small pizza place. I could've sworn that it was real."

"Papers," Henry asked, bewildered. This wasn't Los Angeles.

His father handed him one of the gossip tabloids that Henry was always featured in. And there it was. A picture of him and Kiera. They'd managed to snap pictures of him with a "mystery redhead," or so the headline teased.

He smiled at the picture and handed it back to his father.

"Well, it's not. I'll make sure she knows that her job is safe. Thank you."

His father nodded. "And I'll get your mother to lay off with the matchmaking. She just wants to see you happy. As do I."

Henry didn't say any more. He opened the door to the boardroom for a second time and left. His heart was aching.

He could've sworn that there were feelings between him and Kiera, but he'd been wrong.

And his heart was paying the price.

"Henry! Wait!"

He turned and saw Kiera standing at the end of the hallway. She looked out of breath, her hair was flyaway and her cheeks were bright red from the cold.

"Kiera, what are you doing here?" he said as

he closed the gap. She was still trying to catch her breath.

"Sorry, the cold… I ran."

"I gather that," Henry said. "Why are you here?"

"I'm here for you."

Kiera's heart was racing and she couldn't believe what she was about to do. When she'd been with other men, when the relationship ended, she hadn't really cared.

Except for Brent.

She'd closed off her heart after Brent had broken it. She had gotten on with her life. She had had Mandy, but now she'd let Henry into her heart.

And when she thought he had betrayed her or used her, it had devastated her. Yet, he had asked her to go to California.

He had showed that he cared and she was so scared to move.

So scared to open her heart and take a chance.

Her pulse was racing. She had run all the way to Aspen Grace Memorial. Even though everything was mostly shut down, she still had a pass to the staff entrance and she'd gotten in. She'd just hoped that she wasn't too late and that Henry hadn't left.

And she wasn't too late.

He was still here.

She didn't know what to say.

"You're here for me?" he asked, confused.

She nodded and swallowed the hard lump that had formed in her throat, because she had never said what she was about to say to anyone, except Mandy.

She had never told Dr. Burke that she loved him.

She had never told anyone that she loved them. Not even Brent, because she'd told her parents that when she was small and they'd left her anyway.

It was a huge risk, but Kiera was tired of waiting.

She was tired of being alone.

Tired of waiting for a family that didn't exist. She had to make her own family and that family was Henry.

Henry was her family.

He drove her bonkers and she hated his father and everything his father represented, but she loved Henry.

He was her person.

And she wanted marriage, babies, everything with him. She wanted love, the hurt, the laughter, she wanted everything. She wanted everything she had secretly dreamed about.

He was her everything, and she had been almost stupid enough to let that slip through her fingers because she was a fool.

"I'm here for you." Tears stung her eyes. "This is hard for me to say."

"It's okay," he said gently. "You can tell me anything."

"Okay," she whispered. "Okay."

"You're shaking."

"I know." She smiled and reached up to touch his face, tears rolling down her cheeks. "I love you, Henry. Against every rational fiber in my being, I love you. You made me feel safe in a world where I have never felt safe. I've been using Mandy as a crutch, waiting for people who are never coming back. I've been wasting my life. Holding myself back. I love you."

He smiled at her tenderly. "I love you, too. And I'm sorry."

"For what? You tried to save the hospital. I know that's not your fault."

"No, I'm sorry for not telling you about my past and the debt I owed to my father. I was embarrassed by my mistakes. I still am, but they won't stop me. I don't want to leave you ever."

Her heart soared and tears slid down her cheeks. "I think I need you to kiss me."

"I want to do that, too, but I have something to tell you."

"Oh?"

"The free clinic has been saved. I told my father about us and I threatened to cut ties with him, which would ruin his political career, so he saved the free clinic."

"How?" Kiera asked, taking a step back. "It was bleeding money."

"That night at the fundraiser, you raised a lot more money than you know. The clinic is saved and it's yours if you want it. We can't offer jobs back to everyone who lost their jobs here at Aspen Grace Memorial, but we can hire back quite a few to run that emergency clinic."

"I'm so glad the clinic is saved, but I don't... I don't want it."

Henry raised an eyebrow. "What? I thought that's what you wanted? All this time, fighting with me tooth and nail. The awful signs you made."

Kiera laughed. "It's what I thought I wanted, but it was just something holding me here. I used it as a reason not to leave and not to live my life. You helped me come alive again, Henry. And, I don't want it. Mandy is getting married and moving on... I don't want to be held back. I love you and I want to be with you. And you love California. I've never been to California and I think I would like to go."

"What about Agnes, what about your patients?"

"Agnes will understand and Dr. Carr can take care of her. What I want is you. I want to live my life. Finally. I want to be with you."

She couldn't stop crying as the truth was revealed. She'd spent so much of her life trying to be controlled, trying not to let her emotions show, but it all just came spilling out of her.

"I love you, too, Kiera and I want you. I've held everyone at bay since Michelle died and I used her memory as a shield to keep myself from being hurt again, but then you showed up and got under all those defenses. I fought it as long as I could, but you brought me back to life, too, Kiera. I never thought for a second that you would be the one to bring me back to the land of the living, but you did. And, if you'll have me, I would like to turn our fake engagement into something real?"

"Yes." She smiled. "Yes. I would like that, too."

She threw her arms around him and Henry scooped her up, kissing her. He set her back down on her feet.

"So, I guess this time we can talk about a ring then?"

"A ring?" She laughed. "I don't need a ring."

"Oh, you need a ring now. And I'm not taking no for an answer."

"Should we tell your father it's for real this time?" Kiera asked.

Henry glanced back. "Later. How about we go take Mandy and her fiancé out for dinner? Let's celebrate with your family."

"That sounds like a plan, Dr. Baker. That sounds like a good plan indeed."

They walked out of the empty hospital hand in hand.

Her heart was so full.

And for the first time since being a little girl, she felt like she was finally going home. The family she had longed for, for so long, had finally come to get her.

She was no longer incomplete, frozen and stuck in a holding pattern.

She was whole.

She was going to have a family and a real place to call home.

EPILOGUE

A year later, Huntington Beach, California

THERE WERE NO witnesses except for a justice of the peace who was standing beside him at the edge of the ocean and a small laptop sitting on a table that was connected to another laptop in Aspen, Colorado.

Mandy, Derek and Sif were crowded on the small laptop screen as Henry stood on the beach in the same suit he'd worn the day he met Kiera, exactly one year ago.

They hadn't wanted a big society type of wedding, even though that had been his mother's preference. Henry had been able to keep her at bay by promising her that she could throw a big society event when they headed back to Aspen next week.

One event. That's all Henry was going to give his parents. One photo opportunity. The rest of the time he planned to spend locked away in his Aspen condo with his new bride. This time, she wouldn't be shimmying out of the bed and there would definitely be no pillow walls between them.

It was just going to be the two of them, locked away for a good week.

There would be no work.

No traumas.

No medicine.

Just them.

Kiera walked down the stairs from his beach house. She was wearing a flowing white dress, and an ocean breeze caught it briefly. She laughed and held the dress down as she descended the steps and walked barefoot across the sand toward him.

His heart swelled with pride as he saw her.

Her red hair was braided back, but down, and golden strands shimmered in the bright California sun.

She was absolutely breathtaking.

Once they were in California, she had gotten a job as a trauma surgeon in the best hospital in Los Angeles, and for the last year they had been working hard.

After the ceremony, they were having a nice monthlong vacation, and he was going to make the best of it.

She stood in front of him, smiling.

He took her hands.

"You sure about this?" she asked.

"Positive."

Kiera waved to Mandy and Derek on the screen.

The justice of the peace stepped forward.

"We're gathered here today to witness the union of Henry Terrance Baker and Kiera Micheline Brown. Do you, Henry Terrance, take Kiera Micheline to be your lawfully wedded wife?"

Henry smiled. "I do."

He pulled out a rose gold band that she had picked out from an antique shop in Venice Beach and slipped it on her slender finger.

"And do you, Kiera Micheline, take Henry Terrance to be your lawfully wedded husband?"

"I do." She pulled a simple platinum band out of her dress and slipped it on his finger.

"Then by the power invested in me by the state of California, I now pronounce you man and wife. You may kiss your bride."

Henry smiled, pulled Kiera in close and kissed her, like he'd been wanting to do as he'd counted down the days until they were locked away together in Aspen.

Kiera laughed and blushed.

Henry paid the justice of the peace, who handed them their certificate and then left them alone with their only wedding guests on the laptop.

"Congratulations, you two!" Mandy shouted. "We can't wait until you guys get here tomorrow."

"I'm excited to see you two, as well!" Kiera blew them a kiss and logged off.

Henry picked up the laptop and took his new bride's hands as they stood on the beach together.

"So where do we go for dinner?" he asked.

"I think I'd rather stay in."

He grinned lazily. "Well, you're going to have a whole month of staying in when we get to Aspen."

She cocked an eyebrow. "Is that a threat?"

"You can count on it," he teased, kissing her again. "It's just going to be the two of us on this honeymoon. We'll visit Mandy and Derek, and attend that one event for my mom, but the rest of the time, in our condo, it's just going to be you and me."

Kiera blushed and worried her bottom lip. "About it being the two of us…"

"What?"

"Remember that night a month ago? When we weren't on opposite shifts? That night in the hot tub?"

He grinned. "Yes. I remember that night quite well."

After two months of working opposite shifts, they had finally had a night together and he had taken full of advantage. He'd thought of that night quite often while waiting for their wedding day and monthlong honeymoon. So much so that he had had a hot tub installed at their place in Aspen.

He was going to surprise her with it.

"Well, it's not the two of us anymore."

It took him a moment to let that sink in. "What?"

"I'm pregnant. In about eight months, it's going to be the three of us."

"Are you serious?" he asked.

"Pretty sure. I did several tests because I was kind of shocked. I thought I had the flu, so I had a couple of different swabs while working in the emergency room."

Henry grinned and kissed her. "I'm so happy. We're going to have a baby."

Kiera grinned. "We are. So any kind of hot tub night you have planned in Aspen will have to wait."

"That's fine." He kissed her again and then reached down to touch her belly. "Hot tub time can wait. All I want is you…you two, and we can still have our honeymoon."

She blushed and wrapped her arms around his neck. "We most certainly can. I love you, Henry."

"I love you, too."

And he scooped her into his arms, carrying her up the stairs from the beach to their house to show her exactly what he had in mind for their honeymoon.

What he planned for the rest of their life.

* * * * *